infinite waste

BOOKS BY DEAN F. WILSON

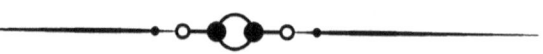

THE CHILDREN OF TELM

The Call of Agon
The Road to Rebirth
The Chains of War

THE GREAT IRON WAR

Hopebreaker
Lifemaker
Skyshaker
Landquaker
Worldwaker
Hometaker

THE COILHUNTER CHRONICLES

Coilhunter
Rustkiller
Dustrunner
Lostlander
Sixshooter
Deadwalker

HIBERNIAN HOLLOWS

Hibernian Blood
Hibernian Charm

AN INFINITE STARS NOVEL

infinite waste

DEAN F. WILSON

Cover illustration by Duy Phan
Icons by Freepik

First Edition 2020

ISBN 978-1-909356-24-5

DIOSCURI PRESS

Published by Dioscuri Press
Dublin, Ireland

www.dioscuripress.com
enquiries@dioscuripress.com

CONTENTS

“

"As people used to be wrong about the motion of the sun, so they are still wrong about the motion of the future. The future stands still, it is we who move in infinite space."

— Rainer Maria Rilke

”

1
wait

The alarms aboard the Starship Gemini were deafening. That's how Skip Sutridge, Captain Exquisite, liked it. He wanted his thoughts drowned in the endless stars. He wanted the panic of his crew to overwhelm his mind, until all that was left was instinct. The instinct to pull the trigger, to push the button, to start a war—or end one.

The Starship Gemini hung in orbit of Sonata V, its twin Infinite engines turned off. It drifted around that blackened globe, burned to a crisp in some ancient battle. The weight of the weaponry on the left rocket made it coast that planet with a slight tilt. The weight of a decision to act rested with Skip alone. He'd been made to share this vessel, but he wouldn't share command of a battle. Maggie Antwa, Commander of Gemini Right, had no authority there.

The space barge came into focus on the viewscreen, with most of it extending far off out of their field of vision. It didn't drift. It sat in the stillness of space, unmoving, exerting a subtle gravity of its own. Its grey metal was shrouded in shadow. Its lights were off. That was always a bad sign. It either meant the crew were dead or they were planning to kill you. More often than not for Skip Sutridge, General Extraordinaire, it was the latter.

"Wait," Maggie said over the intercom. He didn't like her voice, her calm, her certainty. The only surety was in the trigger. Shoot and shoot later. Never ask questions. Never give answers.

"It's a threat," Skip replied through gritted teeth. He kept his finger dangling. The only thing that held it back was the knowledge of how this had panned out last time. His crew were starting to listen to *her*, listen to "reason," whatever that was. He remembered the awe with which they viewed him when he first came on board. That was fading fast.

"We don't know that yet," Maggie pointed out. She liked pointing out things, everything but the enemy's weaknesses. She always wanted to know more, to probe further, to prod deeper. Skip thought a laser could do that just fine.

Even from this far off, Skip could see the giant storage containers piled high across the space barge, held in place with a powerful magnetic hull. It was so potent it tugged even at the Gemini, threatening to separate the twins. Skip almost didn't mind. All the weaponry was on his side of the ship. Only the two giant fighters joined those rockets together, connecting the Infinite engines, letting them travel farther than one alone.

"Just ... give me a minute," Maggie urged. He could hear the beeps of buttons in the background as her fingers worked frantically. Skip only needed one button. As the seconds grew old and died, his finger got a little closer. He wondered how many wars began with gravity.

"There," Maggie said, sending across a report from her scanners. The overlay added a lot of text and faded schematics on the viewscreen, making the colossal space barge look a little less daunting.

"No crew?" Skip asked.

"No life signs."

He didn't like how she said that, as if it meant something else. She was always correcting him. Life had been hell since she boarded. He wouldn't have been surprised if she picked up nothing from him as well.

"What's in the containers?"

More beeps and finger-bashing. "It looks like … some kind of waste."

"Waste?"

"Nuclear."

"Oh."

"Just as well you didn't fire, huh?" Her smug laugh was cut short. "Wait." She always waited. That was her trouble, and she was his.

By the time she noticed the incoming missile, she barely had time to put up the shields on her side of the vessel. It was just as well Skip had noticed. It was just as well he'd fired first.

2
an executive decision

Maggie Antwa hammered her fist down on the shield button. The generators were already primed and ready. Outside, a bubble of energy extended around the most vital parts of Gemini Right: the antennae, the specimen globes, the medical bay, the engine room, the crew quarters. The left rocket—Skip's domain— was left almost entirely defenceless. It was just as well he considered attack the best form of defence.

The missile wormed its way from the space barge towards them, while Skip's answering shot— or questioning shot, even—wiggled along in return. They united in the middle with an explosion that shook the starship, but barely nudged the space barge at all.

"So much for waiting," Skip crooned over the intercom.

Before she could reply, he ended the transmission. She knew what to expect next. No one fired at Skip Sutridge and got away without an answering barrage. If he had to, he'd use up every torpedo he had, and that was a lot. He'd make a lesson out of them. Anyone who knew Skip had learned that lesson early on.

"We've lost steering," her oarsman said.

"I know."

Skip had used his one Executive Star of the month to take over the steering of the entire vessel. She could have used hers to take it back, but she was saving it. Petty vengeance was one of his tactics, not hers. She'd wait.

The Gemini turned about until the left rocket, armed to the teeth, had its port side facing the space barge. The turrets rotated into place. Hatches opened. The volley began. The flak cannons boomed. The blaster rigs sparked. The torpedo bays were emptied. The dark canvas of space was momentarily splattered with light and colour. It was enough to down a lesser vessel, but the space barge was anything but. By the end of it, it seemed like no damage was inflicted at all.

"Are you done?" Maggie asked, forcing open the comms again.

"Never."

"I was going to tell you that they've got shielding."

"I was gonna tell you I don't care."

"It's a waste of weapons."

"Weapons are never a waste, Commander."

"Some of them are, Captain," Maggie said. "That barge isn't commercial. Our latest scans have just come through. I'm sending them over."

"What am I seeing?" Skip asked. He never could read reports. She wondered if he could even read at all.

"It's not just waste, Skip. It's militarised. This is all rigged to blow."

"All the more reason to destroy it."

"It'll destroy itself, and us, and everything else for half the galaxy."

She could hear him grumble. "Why is it here?"

"I don't know."

"Why did they fire at us?"

"I'm not sure. I think it's an automated system. You fired first, so—"

"I always fire first."

"I know."

"We need to know where this is heading," Skip said.

"I agree. I can probably have an analysis done in a few hours."

"That's too long."

"It is what it is."

"I'm going over."

"Are you mad?" She wasn't sure why she asked.

"We've got a powerful weapon sitting in our back yard, Commander. That'll be good for the Empire."

"Or bad for us."

Skip's voice deepened. "Or bad for everyone."

"We should wait. We should investigate."

"Sure thing," he said. "But I'll use my own eyes for that."

3
the offspring

Skip wasted no time explaining himself or justifying his decision. His crew didn't ask him. Even Maggie didn't, though she had done it plenty of times before. He never prepared a defence for such questioning. He just didn't answer. It was even better when he jammed Maggie's signals.

"Do you need a team?" the oarsman of Gemini Left, Lieutenant Larsman, asked. Larsman was a good soldier, but an even better pilot. Skip was confident about leaving him at the wheel.

"I will be fine on my own," Skip replied, heading for the nearest transporter.

Like a good soldier, Larsman didn't argue. He had only served once before with Skip, but he had learned then how well he worked alone. A one-man army, as the slogans often said. The Empire regularly broadcast footage of Skip wading through swarms of enemies, often with a smile on his face, earning him the nickname The Man of No Tears. Skip remembered posing for those shoots. They weren't quite as glorious as they appeared. The battles were fake, but the deaths were real. He wished he could jam the memories.

The transporter took him to the boarding gate of the Offspring, the massive fighter at the front of the vessel. Its wings were clipped at the ends, allowing it to clamp into notches on the sides of both rockets, acting as a bridge between them. There were doors in the wings, and wiring and tubes that connected the fighter's systems to the rockets, allowing each part to support the other.

Before he boarded, he pulled out his datapad and turned on the mirror. This was a little ritual he did before battle, one he rarely told people about, though he was sure many had seen him do it. He stared at his image for a moment, taking in the big, bright eyes, the square jaw and puckered chin, and that suave smile—which was often there even when he wasn't really smiling inside. He tidied up that single blonde curl that hung over his forehead, something he was known for, and was often exaggerated in the posters of him. His hair was thick, but combed neatly, except for that little curl, which he'd had since he was a boy. It was like a little rebellion, an escape from the order of everything else. He thought maybe that was why, despite military regulation, he insisted on keeping it. Some people thought it was narcissism that made Skip complete this little ritual so often, and maybe there was an element of that. Yet, really he was taking one last look so that he could remind himself of who he was, and where he came from. The ranks and armour changed that for many, but he wanted to make certain it never happened to him.

He was about to board when Alex Primus, the sixteen-year-old member of the Empire's celebrated royal family, raced up, panting. He was allowed to board Gemini Left as a favour to his father, who predicted Gemini's voyages would become the stuff of legend—and thus the stuff of status.

"Wait," the teen said, resting against the doorframe.

"I'm kind of busy," Skip said.

"I could come help … if you'd like."

Skip paused. "You?"

Alex looked to the floor. "Yeah."

"I don't think that would be very fitting now, would it? Imagine what the Emperor would say if the royals were suiting up for battle."

"But I can help."

"You're serving the Empire by doing your duty as a royal."

"You mean a puppet."

"I'll pretend I didn't hear that."

Alex clenched his fists. Normally Skip liked to see that in a young man readying for battle, but not now. "That's what all this is, right?" Alex asked. "A pretence."

Skip grabbed Alex by the shoulder. "Cut out that talk, boy. You're dishonouring your name."

Alex shook off Skip's grip and backed away. "You can't dishonour what doesn't have any honour to begin with. It's all a sham. Why can't I fight?"

"Because you don't believe in anything," Skip replied. "You have to have something to fight for."

He turned and boarded the Offspring, quickly sealing the doors as Alex tried to race inside. He could hear the teen mumbling something through the glass. Maybe Alex had to have the last word. Skip often had the last word, usually because the other person was dead.

Skip trotted down the long corridor that led through the wing of the fighter and into the spacious cockpit, with enough space to sleep a dozen people. His Second, Akt Ontri, was there, preparing the vessel for flight.

If there was one person Skip could count on, it wasn't a person at all: it was Akt Ontri. Ontri was an android, more colloquially (and, some would argue, offensively) known as an *aut*, short for *autonomous thing*. He was ninth generation, the most advanced yet, and a bit of an experiment aboard the experiment that was the Gemini. Skip had no illusions that his mission was anything else, but knowing it didn't help with the feeling that he wasn't so much the most celebrated man of the galaxy, but just another guinea pig. He knew what the Emperor might say: *why can't you be both?*

Ontri was humanoid in shape, but didn't look human at all. They'd tried that with seventh generation models, with disastrous results. People didn't like their androids blending in too much, looking too real. It made them uncomfortable. It made it harder to look at them as autonomous things. Most seventh generation auts were destroyed in the so-called Electric Cleansing of 2810, but a few of them were said to be around, in hiding somewhere. It was a crime to harbour one, though some, like Maggie, thought it was a crime to turn them in. It was no wonder she'd gotten on the wrong side of the government. Skip just wondered why he got bundled with her.

"Good sir!" Ontri exclaimed on seeing Skip. That was his familiar, ever-enthusiastic greeting, just for him. The Captain didn't care if it was programmed. Stars, if he could programme all the crew to do it, he'd give the order now.

"Ontri," Skip said. Some people didn't respond to the "pleasantries" of auts, as if the pleasantries of humans were any more real. It always grated on him when he saw a crew member treat Ontri like he wasn't second in command. It reminded him a little too much of his childhood on Alpha Prime, where he was teased for being Rockborn, someone born on one of the galaxy's many asteroid colonies. His family moved to give him a better life, but he had to fight for it. It was no wonder he ended up in the military. No doubt it was a great wonder to the Alphans that he was so good at it too.

Things were much different now. He had Alphans aboard the Gemini, like Larsman. No one dared call him Rockborn now. Few dared defy Ontri either. Skip liked to give his crew a regular reminder that his word was gold up here, and that Ontri spoke his word just as much as he did. He wasn't exaggerating. You couldn't get better programming outside a cult.

"I have prepared your vessel," Ontri said, gesturing towards the controls. Skip and Maggie hadn't come to an agreement on who exactly "owned" the giant fighter at the front of their shared ship, or the even larger fighter-bomber at the back, the so-called Bridge. Those two vessels were what joined the rockets of Gemini Left and Right together, and the only thing that separated their two very different crew. Yet, while no agreement was made, Skip still considered the fighters under his jurisdiction, given he was in charge of the military side of affairs. He made sure Ontri knew that, and, unlike Maggie, Ontri didn't argue at all.

4
punching
through

The Offspring disembarked, unclamping from the rockets on either side. Its thrusters flared up, its engine thrummed, and its outer lights flickered on. And, because it was Skip on board, its weapon systems activated, immediately locking onto the space barge. It didn't require delicate aiming. It'd be hard to miss.

"You're clear to go," Larsman said over the comms. His was one of the few signals Skip was letting through.

"Rolling out," Skip replied.

"You're taking Ontri?"

"I'm not *taking* him. He's coming with me," Skip said.

"I am rather eager to go," Ontri said enthusiastically. There was nothing like a good Emotion Approximation Chip.

"But that leaves me in charge, right?" Larsman asked.

"You've got the wheel," Skip said. That wasn't quite what Larsman wanted to hear, but then Skip didn't want to say it. As far as he was concerned, he was in charge, whether he was on the ship or not. He could've been sipping tea back on Alpha Prime, and he'd still be in charge out here near the Edge, the little-known region at the rim of the Imperius Galaxy, the home of the Pan-Galactic Empire. Skip didn't mind Larsman having the wheel, but not the whole ship.

Skip steered the Offspring towards the space barge. He could really appreciate its size now that he was on an even smaller vessel. By the time he was close, he couldn't see the end of it in either direction. It was like looking at space, if space was a block of metal.

"Are those shields still up?" he asked Ontri.

Ontri was plugged into the ship's computer, getting scanner results sent straight to his processor. One of his eyes flickered as it worked, almost like the robotic equivalent of a twitch. That was one of the things Skip liked about him. For someone, or *some thing*, so artificial, he had those little idiosyncrasies that made him real. He dismissed the technicians' appraisals that they were faults.

"Yes," Ontri said. "Their shields are at ninety-nine point nine nine seven six—"

"Right, I've got it. Prepare the Shield Buster."

The Shield Buster was a specialised weapon designed for punching a small hole through an energy shield, enough to allow a small vessel with a boarding party through (which had earned it the alternative name of Boarder Buster). It was incredibly expensive to make, utilising some of the same fusion technology that powered the Infinite engines. The Gemini only carried two at a time, and had to go back to one of the Core Worlds to restock them. Skip was cautioned to use them wisely, but he didn't go in much for wisdom. He relied on his gut, and his gut used the same language Skip used. It said, "Fire!"

"Primed and armed," Ontri said.

"Bombs away."

Ontri fired the missile, which was loaded under the cockpit. It had its own thrusters and navigational system, and several small auts that lived inside the shell, making small repairs to it as it slowly degenerated from lack of use. Those were sacrificial androids, much like a lot of the soldiers Skip led into battle. You couldn't get too sentimental. It was just the way of things, like the sky was up, like the universe didn't have any directions.

The missile sped towards its target. Answering missiles came out of the space barge, but the auts inside fired smaller missile-destroyers out of tiny ports, ensuring it would reach its destination. It smacked the side of the energy shield with an amplified thud, followed by an electrical wobble as the entire fabric of the shield reacted to the impact. A small wave of energy spread out from the site across the entire shield, highlighting an encasing that would otherwise be difficult to see.

"That'll do it," Skip said.

He pushed hard on the accelerators, sending the fighter through the tiny opening the Shield Buster caused. He knew it would take a few hours to repair the breach. That'd give him plenty of time inside.

The tug of the magnetic hull of the space barge was strong, so strong that he barely needed to clamp into place once he landed on the surface. He used the clamps anyway, just in case the magnetism was turned off. It wouldn't have been the first time Skip was left plummeting. You learned quick in war. If you didn't, you died.

"Cut us a door, please," Skip asked.

Ontri was already on it. He could almost predict Skip's commands. Skip didn't think it was that exceptional, given there were posters and holograms of him all across the galaxy, with his orders used as slogans. He wondered how many children had given a salute before shouting, "Bombs away!" It was amusing, and a little satisfying, to know that Alphan children were emulating his words now. How things had changed.

"I suggest power armour," Ontri said as he assembled his tools to cut through the space barge's hull.

"Yeah, I've got it."

Skip headed to the armoury behind the cockpit. He pulled on the heavy boots, then the motorised metal trousers, with pistons inside to make them move. He donned the bulky chest armour, the great shoulder pads, the huge iron gauntlets. By the end of it, he looked like some kind of mutant with a huge body and a tiny head. This was the armour of the Pan-Galactic Marines, the so-called Heavies. This was as normal to Skip as his everyday clothes. In the Marines, you lived inside your armour. Often, you died in it too.

He stomped out into the cockpit, then down to where Ontri was waiting. He had already cut a hole into the space barge and closed the door of the Offspring to block the way, just in case.

"Safety first," Ontri said, tapping one of his tools off Skip's helmet.

"Now," Skip said, placing his helmet on. It made a hiss as the pressure changed inside. "Time to find out what we've got sittin' out here on the Edge."

5
one heart beating

Skip stepped aboard the space barge. His armoured boot made a clang that echoed through the dark corridors ominously. He was never one for stealth, but his gut told him he might need it now. It told him he'd need that armour too.

He sealed the hatch behind him, but didn't remove his helmet. His visor showed the air was breathable, but he didn't always trust technology. If there was one thing he had learned time and time again on the battlefield, it was not to lose your helmet. The renowned Admiral Mendan Ennas had learned that too, though a bit too late. That probably explained his madness.

He jammed Maggie's incoming signals. No doubt she was berating him. He didn't need to hear her to know how it'd go. He'd heard it plenty of times before. He needed no distractions now. He needed to focus. That's how you got the kill.

The corridor of the space barge was completely black, darker even than space. At least there were stars out there. Only the glow of the light in his visor illuminated the area around him, and that was faint. There was something about the darkness here that seemed different, like maybe it was staring back.

He turned on the flashlight attached to his right arm and held it before him. The light showed what seemed like a never-ending hexagonal corridor, metal plated on all sides. The plating was the same throughout, so you weren't fully sure if you were standing on the floor or the ceiling. It was like being out in space. It was a little bit disorientating.

Skip strolled through, moving his arm in a circle before him, getting that light into all the corners, burning away the darkness. He couldn't help but think of the tales his father used to tell him as a kid about the Umbra, those so-called creatures of shadow. He knew better now than to flinch at boogeymen, but something about this shade set him on edge. Just as he burned away the darkness, something about the darkness burned away his courage.

"Skip," a voice said suddenly.

He jumped inside the armoured suit. He was glad its weight didn't make it jump too. The sound would have echoed for days.

"Stars, Maggie," he grunted. "How did you through?"

"You can't jam me forever, y'know."

"I can try."

"It's not good for you."

"So's a lotta things."

"I mean, it's not wise. You're all alone out there."

"If I'm alone, then I'm fine."

He waited for her to make some quip about

him only needing himself to get into trouble. He was preparing his retort, which might have involved listing all the awards he'd won—by his lonesome, mind—and how really any apparent "trouble" he got into was just a demonstration of how to get out of it. Or something like that.

"Don't be so certain about anything over there," Maggie said finally. "I'm running several tests right now. I'll have the reports—"

"Oh, enough of your reports."

He jammed the signal again. He used Admiral Ennas' technique for that. He was the one who taught him that the first call of action in a war should be to cut communications. Silence was as much a weapon as it was a shield. That's what worried him about the space barge. It was altogether silent.

Part of him, a part he'd thought he'd killed off years ago with training, wanted to reopen communication with the Gemini. He had a channel ready for Ontri, but he had a feeling Maggie would be waiting for him on the other end of that as well. No doubt she was working frantically to get back in touch with him, to send him on some more reports. There were wars that were won and lost while people were writing reports. The only report he cared about was the one that said "Victory."

He continued through the ship, hammering his gauntleted fist against access pads beside the hexagonally-shaped doors (which also looked the same no matter which way was up). Most of the doors were sealed tight, and probably for good reason. If this ship really was full to the brim with nuclear waste, he hoped to the stars he couldn't get through so easily. Even his entry aboard the barge was a little too effortless, as if someone had let him in. He didn't like that. He'd rather fight his way aboard.

There was a sound like scurrying feet behind him. He turned as fast as the heavy suit would allow, barely catching a glimpse of something darting into the shadow.

It looked like he might get his fight after all.

6
First contact

Skip grabbed the blaster from his left hip. He aimed it down the corridor, into the darkness, at the darkness. He brought the torch light up slowly, knowing that as soon as he revealed whatever was hiding there, the battle would commence. It had to happen at the right moment. The right moment was when his finger hit the trigger.

As soon as the light illuminated a hunched-over figure with broad shoulders and a gnarled head, he fired. It didn't matter who or what it was. Skip had been in too many wars to let sentiment slow him down.

But the laser blast missed, leaving a charred mark on the wall instead. His aim was right, but the creature was quick. He only knew it was a creature by how it ran towards him, bounding down on all fours. It dived, right into the blast of a second bolt. Its snarl was ear-piercing. It curled into a ball as soon as its body hit the floor.

Skip took a careful step forward, shining his torch on the creature, and keeping his blaster pointed there too. It was hard to tell what it was. It almost looked like a mutated rat, which hadn't just grown big, but had a grown a little human too. Skip was well used to hybrids at this stage. The galaxy was full of them. But he hadn't encountered, or even heard of, something like this.

"You," he said, kicking one of its paws. It curled up tighter. "What *are* you?" Skip added. "Are there more of you on board?"

Skip had barely finished the sentence when he heard a flurry of feet behind him. He turned, slowed by his power suit, to see two more of the rat-men diving at him, claws slashing. They seemed to have had artificial blades added to their hands to enhance each stab and slash. They clanged with fury against the metal of Skip's suit.

He stumbled backwards, his back striking the wall. As he lifted the blaster up, one of the rat-men knocked it from his hand. The other tried to break the glass on Skip's mask, driving the knife-like claws straight against the visor. Skip was glad it was reinforced, but their blades seemed to be reinforced too. Each strike left a little pocket in the glass, which obstructed Skip's vision.

The creatures were so close, clinging to his body, that Skip had no room to use another weapon. He swung with his armoured fists, striking one of the creatures straight in the jaw. He could hear the crunch as metal met with bone. The creature fell backwards, then scurried off into the darkness, howling as it went. Skip didn't like that—not because he felt bad for the fiend, but because howling creatures tended to come back with more.

The other rat-man disappeared from his vision

for a moment, but he could hear its frantic steps. Skip turned to find it reaching for his fallen blaster. He threw himself at it, and it took all his strength to jump in that armour. The weight of it came down on the creature just as it pointed the blaster. He crushed it into the ground, hearing the snap of ribs and its muted, blood-clogged cry.

Skip struggled to push himself up and get back to his feet. He remembered Admiral Mendan's frequent caution: *Don't you damn fall over in that, unless it's right into your grave.* It only took a few seconds to get back up, but it only took a few seconds to kill you too.

Skip yanked the blaster from the rat-man's claw, putting it back into its holster. He pulled a bigger gun from his back: a plasma rifle. Then he turned back to where the other creature fled. He followed it into the darkness, expecting to see it curled up in the corner, licking its wounds or playing dead. He couldn't find it at all.

He continued on, deeper and farther, until the shadow swallowed the dead and wounded rat-men behind him. He could still hear the faint moan of the first creature, until the overwhelming silence of the ship swallowed that too.

He reached a barred door at the end. Beside it was a keypad with a blinking light. Skip tapped the side of his helmet, close to his left temple. A faded image of Ontri appeared in his visor, with one of the puck marks obscuring the robot's right eye.

"What can I do for you, good sir?" Ontri asked in his usual over-polite way.

"Get me a code for this, will ya?" Skip sent an

image of the keypad over.

"Acquiring."

"Acquire quicker, if you can." Skip knew that some auts performed the same all the time, but Ontri could overclock himself. He'd burned out his circuits a few times before by doing it, but on most occasions he got better results in half the time. Skip had a feeling he needed every second he could get.

"Acquired," Ontri said.

The code immediately appeared in his visor. Skip tried to delicately tip the numbers on the pad with his armoured index finger. The pad beeped a failure notice twice as he hit the wrong digits.

"Do you require aid, Captain?" Ontri asked.

"I require smaller bloody fingers," Skip growled. He holstered the plasma rifle and pulled off his right gauntlet. He flexed his fingers, then bashed the code in swiftly. The door beeped and opened.

Skip didn't realise that he'd gasped.

"Do you require aid, Captain?" Ontri repeated.

The visor wasn't big enough to see everything. There must have been hundreds of those creatures in the next room, many of them labouring over gigantic nuclear torpedoes. Many others were lined up near the door, some of them with claws, others with guns.

Skip hammered his fist down on the keypad, shutting the door firmly.

"I need an army," he said.

7
on the run

Despite his natural bravado, Skip knew when to fight and when to run. There was a big difference between being brave and being suicidal. Some said Skip was a little bit of both. Others preferred to use the word "homicidal."

He ran, thundering back down the corridor, slowed by the weight of his armour. Sometimes soldiers didn't get a choice at all. With that armour, they couldn't run.

He heard the door open behind him, but he couldn't glance back. Instead, he tapped his index and middle fingers of his right hand against his left wrist, where camouflage markings on the armour indicated some touch panels. A camera on the back of his helmet turned on, and his visor displayed the image of a dozen rat-men charging along behind him.

He kept running, but now he moved his right fist in a circle beneath his left forearm, which triggered another piece of his armour: the shoulder-mounted gun. A hatch opened in the large shoulder pad, and a small turret rose from it. It swivelled around, automatically locking onto its first target.

"Full auto," Skip said with a pant. That was

another thing about running. Sometimes the heaving and huffing made those voice commands hard to register. Like now.

The gun sat idle, while the first bolts from the enemy came in, pinging off the armour, searing the walls.

Skip gulped down his breath. "Full. Auto," he repeated more forcefully, articulating the words better, pronouncing them more slowly.

The turret kicked into action, firing a flurry of bolts at its first target before immediately moving on to the next. It didn't wait for the kill like a human might. It assumed it got it. There was no room for doubt with machines. It was what made Ontri such a valuable ally—and such a dangerous one.

Skip didn't slow down. He leapt—so much as the armour would let him leap—over the fallen rat-man that had started this whole mess. He was still playing dead, but he would only be playing for so long. Skip wasn't even sure it was a he, but it helped. It was easier to kill men. And if they were rodents too? Well, that just made it damn simple.

He bounded down the corridor, skidding at the corner and crashing into the wall. Then he was off again, darting down the next passage, and the next. Not a single panel on the walls or floor or ceiling looked remotely different. Only the doors gave it any distinction. Maybe it was designed that way on purpose. Invaders would get instantly lost.

Skip wasn't sure what turn to take to make it back to his ship. He let his gut guide him. That had proved reliable in the past. Yet, everything failed you some time. Today was the day for Skip. Something told him he had taken the wrong turn, but there was no time to change that now. The gunfire behind him was growing stronger, despite the dozens of slain rat-men his shoulder-mounted turret left in his wake.

He opened the comms to Ontri. "Get me a route out of here, will ya?"

"Acquiring."

"Stars, I need it now!"

It didn't matter that the gunfire could be heard on the comms. Ontri's Emotion Approximation Chip was just a series of algorithms that simulated responses to certain detected situations, based on a variety of parameters. He didn't register the "urgency" of the situation like Maggie might—but he wouldn't say "I told you so" either.

Yet, Ontri was designed first and foremost to learn. He had learned a variety of phrases that the good Captain would use that boiled down to asking him to overclock himself. "I need it now" was one of them. He ramped up his processor speeds significantly, working through the data more quickly. Something popped as he did this, but it seemed to have zero bearing on the outcome.

"Acquired," Ontri droned. "Sending now."

Part of the route lit up in the overlay of the ship in Skip's visor, with a blinking red dot where he was, and not a single blinking light behind him. Skip never fully trusted technology, and this was a good reason why. He could still see the blasts of energy in the corners of his eyes and still hear the scamper of rodent feet behind him.

"Why aren't we picking up vitals?" he asked, taking the next right, then left, then left again. He hammered his fist against a marking on his thigh, which triggered an adrenaline injection. He needed it.

"They appear to have some kind of vitals dampener," Ontri explained in his usual matter-of-fact manner.

"Can you—?"

"Already on it, sir."

Suddenly the visor displayed a lot of other blinking yellow dots behind him. A few of them vanished into the darkness, but it seemed there was always more to fill their places. Skip had been in fights like this before, but usually with bigger guns. Even then, there was always a constant worry: that he'd run out of ammunition before they ran out of bodies.

"By my estimates," Ontri said, "the quickest and safest route is to circle around at the next right." A new route displayed in grey, circling back around to where he came from. "You will lead most of the enemy around the square, but you will face heavy resistance once you cross over old territory."

"Yeah, I guessed that."

"A suggestion, Captain."

"Fire away," Skip said. He suddenly thought better of that wording. "I mean, go ahead."

Ontri's voice came through crackled, then cut off entirely. Then a sudden, sharp pain pierced through Skip's head. He felt like his brain was on fire. The static in his ears increased until it was like the roar of speakers. He stumbled, grasping at his helmet, cringing from the pain.

He fell, and everything seemed to go black for a moment. When it faded moments later, he saw a furry foot in front of his visor. He glanced up to see a robed rat-man, hunched over like the rest of them, but taller and broader, and leaning on a mechanical staff.

"You and your weapons," the figure growled.

Something ripped the turret from his shoulder. It had long ran out of ammunition.

"Well," the figure added, before the stabbing pain began anew. "We have ours."

8
the wrong kind of waiting

Maggie worked tirelessly to try to override the jam on Skip's signal, but it proved fruitless. Any of the techniques she tried would have worked in normal circumstances, but she knew Skip's reputation more than she knew him: if he wanted to disappear, he'd disappear. He had only returned to the Pan-Galactic Empire a year ago, and she'd heard the whispers that he'd returned changed. They called him the Man of No Tears, the most celebrated man of the Empire, more popular than the Emperor himself. Maggie wondered how many people Skip had left crying.

"What'll we do?" her Second, Toz Ilgi, asked. Skip had the definition of loyalty in his Second, but Toz was a different sort altogether: a hired hand. He'd worked with Maggie before, back in the days when she ran the Ensemble of Environmentalist Elders, or the EEE. Toz was good at getting into places, though not so good at getting out. He was paying the same penance she was: "galaxy service" aboard the flagship of the Empire. It mightn't have even seemed like a punishment, were it not for Skip. She wasn't quite shackled to him, but her ship was chained to his.

"Keep probing," Maggie said. "I need a walk."

She left the command room and strolled through the brightly-lit corridors of Gemini Right, putting her bushy, brown hair up into a bobbin as she went. She passed several pod rooms, where double doors sealed in artificial habitats, part of her research work on the vessel (all fuelling the scientific efforts of the Empire). She wasn't given time as a sentence. She was given a goal. Ten monumental discoveries. She had her definition of what "monumental" meant, but the Empire had its own. From the outside of the ship, the pods looked like glass bubbles stuck to the hull, each housing its own unique environment. There was one with snow, one with water, one like a jungle, one like a desert. She didn't need planets. She brought them with her.

She passed by the medical bay, where three of Skip's soldiers were still being treated for burns from the last "mission," if it could be called that. People said he was more tactical before his disappearance. It seemed like he was getting more and more reckless by the day. That wouldn't be so bad if the lives of four hundred crew members weren't at stake. There was no medical bay on Gemini Left. Skip had had the old one converted into an armoury. That whole ship was just a drifting array of weapons. Maggie had a feeling that Skip considered his crew to be weapons too.

She went to Engineering, where Cada Tybar was holed up. She was one of the most gifted mechanics Maggie had ever met. In the three months since the Gemini launched, she had already pushed the Infinite engines beyond known capacity, allowing them to travel farther into space, out to the Edge. Some explorers had been out there before, but they knew they would never make it back. They let capsules with their maps and data gradually drift to the centre of the galaxy, to civilisation, while the pioneers were lost to the unknown. In many ways, Cada was partly to blame for the current mess. Were it not for her work, they wouldn't be out this far. They wouldn't have encountered that space barge.

"We could dock and board," Cada said before Maggie had a chance to talk.

"No. Skip's doing the exploring."

"That's madness."

"Yeah, but it's probably safer that way."

"Not for him."

"For us."

A light blinked on the data pad on Maggie's left wrist. She tapped it, revealing a small hologram of Toz, looking as trapped as ever. "What's up?" she asked.

"We've got a problem," Toz said.

He transferred a signal to the larger screen in Engineering. Maggie expected to see Skip. Instead, she saw some kind of hybrid of man and rat, leaning heavily on a glowing staff. It didn't look like it glowed from any known light source.

"We've got your Captain," the creature said.

The camera panned down, and there was Skip, bruised, bloodied and dazed. And someone's prisoner. Not like Maggie expected at all.

9
the language barrier

Skip was subdued. It wasn't a position he was in often, and not one that suited him. He wasn't just the Man of No Tears—he was the Man Who Didn't Kneel. Yet there was a first time for everything. He was stripped of his armour, with his arms tied behind his back, with the golden curl that so many identified him with now straightened out with sweat. He looked like a wounded man, a broken man. He even looked like that to himself, for he saw his faint reflection in the glass of the camera that was pressed close to his face.

"I am As-hamaz," the rat-man sneered. "I am your Captain now. Abandon your posts. Leave your vessel for us. If you do it willingly, we will grant you mercy and let six of you take an escape pod to wherever the galaxy leads you. All others will be slaves to the Raetuumaka."

The other rat-men cheered and chanted, speaking some other tongue which Skip's implanted auto-translator didn't recognise. It tried hard to work out the grammar and syntax, to approximate a translation, but all that came back was "Error. Unrecognised.

Attempting deconstruction." He hadn't yet heard enough of their language for the translator to work on, but he had a feeling he'd be hearing a lot more soon enough.

"We will comply," Maggie said. Skip was horrified to hear her surrendering already, but then he wasn't sure what he expected from her. She wasn't a military girl. She didn't understand the concept of "No surrender." She even led starship rallies throughout key sectors in protest against the Empire's policy of letting troops fight to the last bullet and breath instead of working out some means of peace.

As-hamaz grinned, showing his sharpened teeth and long, forked tongue, which he waved like a flag of victory. His whiskers twitched with satisfaction. He rested less on his staff, didn't stoop so low, and held his furry chin on high.

"But," Maggie added, and it was to Skip like an opening volley. "But you must hand our Captain … I mean, our former Captain … over to us first. I choose him to be one of the six to take the escape pod."

Good, Skip thought. *Now I see it.* The trick.

As-hamaz saw it too. He snarled and grabbed Skip by the scruff of the neck.

"He's *ours* now. For attacking the Raetuumaka, he shall suffer the Dozen Deaths. This is the law of our people. This is the will of the Raetuu. There is *no* negotiation."

"It is *our* law that our Captain always be the first to take an escape pod," Maggie lied. In fact, it was the opposite. The Captain was supposed to go down with the ship, not that it always transpired that way. Some were too valuable, either for their expertise or their image—or, in Skip's case, both.

As-hamaz cut the transmission. Skip wondered what Maggie made of that. It wasn't the first time Skip had seen a transmission cut in such a tense situation. Sometimes he did it himself. It often paid to play hard ball, to seem like it was all or nothing. The problem was knowing just how far you could go before it was nothing at all.

The rat-man, who might have been some kind of rat-king for all Skip knew, turned to his comrades and spat a series of commands to them in that harsh tongue of theirs. Each new sentence gave Skip's auto-translator something extra to work on, but it still wasn't enough.

"Maybe I can help," Skip suggested.

As-hamaz turned to him and drew in close, close enough that his whiskers tickled Skip's face. He smelt the foul breath and wondered what those creatures ate. He tried not to wonder too deeply.

"Go on," As-hamaz said.

"Maybe I can reason with her."

"Reason? No. There are laws to follow. We have ours, and you have yours. You must face the Dozen Deaths, and yet she must make you take the escape pod first. How do we reconcile this? It must be reconciled."

"Tell me the name of your law," Skip said, "in your tongue."

As-hamaz squinted his eyes. "Daedel Itkua."

"And what would you call me in … you know, whatever it is you speak?"

"In Raetuum, you are Daedes."

"The dead?" Skip guessed.

"Soon to be," As-hamaz snarled.

The rat-man turned back to his associates, rattling off more commands. Skip's auto-translator worked furiously, using the extra words and translation Skip had acquired, until finally it had developed an approximate dictionary of their language, with a basic understanding of their grammar. It constantly updated as they spoke.

"Destroy their escape pods," As-hamaz ordered in Raetuum.

"But then none of them can leave," another replied.

"Exactly. Then our laws are reconciled."

He turned back to the camera, signalling with his claw. The image of Maggie, more tense than ever, came on. The waves of her bushy, brown hair took up most of the screen, along with her big, blue eyes, wide with apprehension.

"I think we got off—"

"We've found a solution," As-hamaz said with glee.

Skip saw the rat-men heading to their gun-chambers. He saw in Maggie's face that she would try to negotiate, but there was no negotiation. Already the offer of six people saved was off the table. Everyone would die or become slaves.

"Good," Maggie said. "We are happy to reach some kind of compromise."

"Retreat!" Skip shouted.

Maggie's face looked more surprised than ever.

"It's a lie," Skip said. "Get out of here, Mags! Full throttle!"

As-hamaz knocked off the screen and smacked Skip across the mouth.

He spat blood. "That all ya got?"

As-hamaz snarled. "I'm saving your lives for the Dozen Deaths. But let's not save them any longer. Let's get started with the first one."

10
a hard turn

Maggie immediately issued a Code Yellow command to both sections of the Gemini, followed swiftly by a video recording of Skip's desperate plea. She had to do this for his troops, because she knew they would never follow her direction otherwise. As demoralising as it was, she needed them to focus on getting away.

The large fighter-bomber that joined the rear of both rockets, dubbed the Bridge, broke off, controlled by an Automated Auxiliary Android, or AAA, which powered up and left its alcove to take the wheel. The right rocket began to turn, while the left drifted for a moment as the crew there were somewhat panicked by seeing their Captain taken.

Maggie took the nearest transporter, which brought her straight to the command room. Axel Hoodan was at the wheel, gesturing dramatically over the motion-controlled grid. The rocket turned slowly in response.

"Get our shields up," Maggie told her Second.

Toz was already working on it, but Maggie raced over to one of the tactical stations on either side and started powering up some of the shields herself. There were dozens of them throughout the vessel, all independent from one another, an idea she and Cada came up with in case of a cyber attack or power outage. It was safer that way, but it also took longer to get all those shields online.

The vessel rocked as a turret on the space barge opened fire. The blasts struck the shields guarding some of the environmental modules, which the attackers must have mistaken for escape pods.

"We've lost ten percent shields," Toz said. He manned the other tactical station, rerouting power from the shields on the other side of the vessel.

"Get us out of here, Axel!" Maggie barked.

"I'm trying!" Axel moved quicker than before, but nothing could speed up the turning of such a large vessel. He'd given as much power as possible to the thrusters. Anything else would need to come from the shields.

Another volley hit, rocking the vessel. They gave it their all, stealing power from unessential systems, throwing everything at the thrusters. Axel was a pantomime on stage, arms waving madly, watched only by the stars outside. Everyone else was glued to their respective screens.

All they could do was turn and try to flee, holding up the shields for as long as they could. They couldn't fire back. There were no weapons on Gemini Right. Everything was on the other side.

Then a shadow passed over the entire room, and Maggie turned to see the other rocket cruising past. It moved between her vessel and the space barge, with its own turrets turning in place. She could hear the rounds of flak fire as it drifted through. Then she saw the fiery, smoking ruins of the guns on the space barge, and some smaller pockets of smoke trailing behind Gemini Left. It moved faster than her vessel, because no energy was being routed to the shields. Everything was put into the thrusters and weapons.

Axel relaxed his frantic arms, but the moment of victory was short-lived. No sooner did the crew of her ship smile before it was wiped clean off their faces. Hatches opened up across the space barge, out of which flooded dozens of fighters.

11
against
programming

Maggie issued the same command to the Offspring, where Ontri sat patiently, completely unfazed by the events that were transpiring. The command triggered a set reaction: to follow it to the letter. Yet, when he saw the video footage of Skip's distress, his Emotion Approximation Chip triggered a different reaction: to defy that command. He was torn between the conflicting information, but unlike humans, he immediately calculated a resolution.

He gently pressed the Auto button on the touchscreen before him, then stood up as the closest AAA aboard the Offspring powered up. A hidden door in the wall opened, revealing an alcove in which the android was stored. Ontri paused and cocked his head as it passed him. He was naturally curious about all beings, but he wondered about auts more than most. He even wondered if he was made to wonder, and if maybe, deep down, on perhaps a microscopic level, the other races had their own kind of wiring and coding too.

He strolled to the hatch door, naturally adjusting

to the shifting of the fighter as the AAA started to steer it off at an angle. Ontri performed a quick scan for life aboard the vessel, a requirement of his Preservation Chip, before opening the door to the vacuum of space. He leapt out, and the force of the space barge's magnetic hull yanked him towards it, until he struck with a clang.

If he could breathe, he would have taken a deep breath. Then he calculated his next move, faced with the biggest wonder of all: how he would rescue the good Captain Sutridge.

12
death by a thousand stings

The Gemini rockets flew roughly parallel, each one taking over the other a little, both crew desperately trying to align them, while even more desperately trying to escape from the approaching swarm of fighters. The Bridge hovered over both rockets, waiting for the opportune time to clamp into place. The Offspring, on the other hand, lagged behind, trailed by the swarm.

"Get us out of here!" Maggie shouted.

"I can't power up the Infinite engines until our fighters dock," Axel replied.

Maggie turned back to the screen, where the blinking blue dot that marked the Offspring seemed to vanish in a sea of red. The enemy was everywhere. If both fighters weren't locked together with the rockets, they would be left behind when hitting warp speeds. The rockets would also travel significantly slower when flown independently.

Maggie tried to open up the comms to Ontri, but it was blocked. Then she tried Lieutenant Larsman, who she knew was always eager to get up close and personal with the enemy.

"We're busy here!" Larsman replied. He was steering the ship with his left hand and manning a remote gun station with his right. You could tell, because he gritted his teeth and roared as he rattled off his shots. Some called him the Octopus, because he'd be manning eight stations at once. Skip might've been a one-man army, but Larsman was a one-man crew.

"I need you to take over the Offspring," Maggie said. "Ontri's not answering, and … I think it needs a human touch."

"I'm game," he replied. "Here, Drom. Take the wheel."

Even when Drom came over, Larsman kept firing away. Maggie wasn't all that surprised. With Skip's crew, it was hard to peel them away from a battle. She wondered if they'd keep on shooting even after they were dead. She had a feeling she might know the answer soon enough.

The Offspring headed straight for the Gemini, taking evasive action as it went. The AAA routed shields to the rear and made no effort to fire back. The command Ontri left was to get back to the ship as soon as possible. It was getting there, but not soon enough.

Larsman's grizzled face appeared on the screen. "You're relieved."

The AAA immediately left its station and returned to its alcove, where it powered down. It made no assessment of the risk it faced there, of the raging battle outside. There were humans who wished they could turn off so easily.

Larsman took over the controls, taking a hard left, leading half the fighters around after him. He dove down, then pulled up sharply, performing a loop until he was behind enemy lines. He rattled off the guns, tearing through two of the fighters before he flew through the blaze. The debris clattered off the shields and bounced away into some of the other fighters. That was one of the few good things about fighting a swarm. With a bit of luck, taking out some would inadvertently take out others too.

The bad part was that there were many more to take their place.

Aboard Gemini Left, Larsman toyed with the controls. He remembered his first drone as a child, which he flew over government territory, taking photos along the way. That was when he saw the bigger drones, the bigger ships. That was when he wanted to fly those. Steering the Offspring was easy, like a dance, not like the unresponsive rocket. There was no space ballet with that.

He zig-zagged through the crowd of fighters, spinning here, rolling there. He fit through spaces others wouldn't have dared fly through, and dodged the undodgeable. It was all second nature to him. He could do it in his sleep—and often did. That was why he got bored so easily, why he so often ended up pulling over a second or third console to do something else.

He did that now, reaching for a gun station, keeping one eye pinned to the screen. His finger touched the edge of the flak cannon's trigger, but the explosion he saw was on the Offspring. His jaw almost dropped as the fighter halted suddenly.

"What happened?" Maggie asked over the comms.

"Damn!" he said. "The controller's been hit. I've lost control."

The Offspring was a sitting duck.

13
unbreakable

The Raetuumaka dragged Skip away and cast him into a holding cell, binding his hands in an energy ball. He could stretch his fingers inside, but he couldn't touch or grasp anything outside the globe. Some "energy magicians", like the galaxy famous Parahoudini, claimed to be able to get out of those cuffs, but it was all games and tricks. This was altogether real.

"Human, I guess," a voice said from the shadows in the corner. Skip didn't like when shadows seemed to move or talk. It made those childhood tales of the Umbra feel a little real as well.

"Who's there?" Skip asked. He would have rather asked it with a gun.

The figure leaned forward, letting the light reveal its snout and whiskers. It was a rat-man, just like the rest of them, though its hands were sealed in an energy ball too.

"I am El-erae," she said. Skip wasn't sure why he assumed it was a she, but she spoke a little softer than many of the others, and had softer features too. Her fur was a light brown, with a patch of white across one eye. "The Outcast," she added.

"What'd you do?"

El-erae gave a meek smile. "No introduction then?"

"I don't do introductions."

"Just partings?"

"If I have a weapon, then yeah."

"Maybe you will get on with my kin."

Skip held up his bound hands. "Yeah, I don't think so."

El-erae leaned closer. "What did *you* do?"

"Came lookin' where I wasn't wanted, I guess."

El-erae nodded solemnly, as if she understood well what that was like.

"And might have killed a hundred or two," Skip added.

El-erae didn't nod to that.

"What about you?" Skip asked. "Eat someone else's cheese?"

"I existed."

Skip tutted. "Been there. Stars, been there my whole life. But see, I'm one o' the lucky ones, because when I break the rules, I often get rewarded for it."

"Except now," El-erae observed.

Skip grumbled. "Now's not over yet. That's the good thing about now."

"You might wish it was. You have the energy brand of one facing the Dozen Deaths." She gestured above Skip, and he noticed for the first time a faint glowing sigil above his head. He didn't recognise the symbol. It must have been part of the Raetuum tongue.

"I've faced more than a dozen in my time," Skip replied.

"And lived?"

"Well, what do *you* think?"

"I make no assumptions any more. I have lived to see ghosts stalk ships and shadows consume worlds. Once I prayed to the Blinking Gods in the sky, but when I came up here, I found that they were far more distant, that when it came to our troubles, they were blind."

"So, you're one of *those*," Skip said.

"One of what?"

"A ... believer."

"I believe in evil."

"Do you now?"

El-erae nodded emphatically. "I believe it has taken over my people, that it is using them to orchestrate the devastation of worlds."

"Just like Sonata V," Skip said, recalling the scorched surface.

"No," El-erae said, and her eyes grew grim. "Your people destroyed that."

14
something
tactile

Maggie raced to the nearest transporter, taking it straight to the docking bay that led to the Bridge. She entered through the door in the right wing, which was sealed tightly to an entrance on the rear of Gemini Right. The seal was so seamless that it was hard to tell where the two vessels, or parts of the larger vessel, began or ended.

She relieved the AAA, who was perched motionless in the driver's seat, and took the ship off automatic. She fiddled with the touchscreen for a moment, gritting her teeth as she struggled to get to grips with it. She reached beneath the desk and pulled a lever. The touchscreen flipped, revealing a set of joysticks in good old-fashioned leather. That was how she'd learned to fly on her father's farm. She still had it etched into her memory, in both her mind and her hands.

She released the clamps holding the fighter-bomber in place, and watched as the rockets on either side seemed to drift away. She powered up the thrusters, which packed a punch, pushing her vessel harder and faster than they did on the heavier rockets. She would have loved to have had some time to adjust to the controls, to give it a test flight, a few turns and twirls. But there was no time for tests, and there was nothing like the real thing.

She turned sharply, heading for where the majority of the swarm were converging: where the Offspring was slowly rotating around on the spot. That was the problem with AAAs. Until they were given a command, they would just sit there, waiting. The four auts aboard the Offspring were still dozing in their alcoves, oblivious to the battle outside. There should have been five aboard, Maggie thought. She wondered why Ontri had stopped responding, and seemed to be making zero effort to fly away. She couldn't pick up his signal on the fighter, but she presumed it was because of Skip's signal block. He didn't want her getting through, which was fine, but Maggie feared it might cost him his rescue.

She gave the engines everything—everything bar her life. As the tiny specks of the swarm turned into larger fighters on the viewscreen, she had a feeling she might have to give that too.

She scanned the approaching ships. There were no life signs, but then her scans of the space barge produced the same results. Maybe those fighters were empty, controlled from afar, or steered by auts, but Maggie couldn't take the chance. She was going to do this her way, which meant taking no lives. Skip was "all guns blazing," but Maggie was "think first, shoot never." She believed first and foremost in the redemption of all, that everything had a place and a purpose, if they could all just find a way to get along. She only hoped that the enemy would see it, and realise she wasn't an enemy at all.

They didn't.

The first wave of ships bypassed the spinning Offspring altogether, much to Maggie's surprise, and came straight for her. She wasn't sure why, and she had no time to find out. She pulled up quick and performed a barrel roll, one of her favourite moves as a child. It was something else entirely inside a fighter-bomber. Even with the g-force stabilisers on, she could feel the weight of the ship as it swung around. That was something you missed with remote flying. It didn't have the same feel, and thus you didn't react the same way at all.

Larsman's image came on her screen. "Stars, Maggie, why didn't you let me steer?"

"You got your chance."

"Not in person."

"You'd have killed."

"Your point?"

"I can do it without killing."

"Good luck with that, Maggie." He paused. "Stars, good luck to us all."

15
battle without battle

Maggie armed the torpedoes, which gave her a sick feeling in her stomach. Her fingers hovered over the trigger buttons. She knew that with just a little push, she could end the lives of many. It was a power she didn't like to wield, a power that didn't suit her. For whatever reason, it wasn't so easy to save lives.

She fired.

The torpedoes launched from beneath the hull, close to the wings. Their speed made them difficult to shoot down, and the explosion would still cause tremendous damage. She watched as they snaked through the inkwell of space, straight towards where the swarm was heading. She clenched her eyes, waiting for the moment of the strike. She could see the explosion behind her eyelids, and feel the shockwave rock her vessel. When she reopened her eyes, she saw where it had made its mark, several metres in front of the oncoming fighters. The shockwave knocked them back, disabling some and sending others spinning. Not a single one was destroyed, and no lives were lost either.

Maggie was a woman of science, of experiment, and this was an experiment that had proven results. She could fight, and use weapons of war, in a different way than anyone else had tried. And maybe, just maybe, she could win.

She launched a second set of torpedoes, farther off, blocking the advancement of a second wave of fighters. Whether it was natural or artificial intelligence inside those vessels, they had learned from the first attack and now veered off sharply. Few were caught in the shockwave. That was the thing about science. Your enemy could learn it too.

So she changed the torpedo pattern, sending some out wide, making others loop. She was able to redirect a few manually, letting them make a flight path for the fighters to detect, before radically changing it. Others she shot down herself, causing the explosion early, throwing off the enemy. In time, they didn't know what she was doing, and couldn't get through the seemingly endless wall of explosions that blocked their advance.

They turned to regroup, possibly forming their own new plan of attack. That was Maggie's window of opportunity. She blasted forward towards the Offspring and hovered over it. She fired magnetic tow cables down. They were meant for cargo, not ships, but they gripped the hull of the Bridge all the same. The Offspring shook as the weight of the larger fighter-bomber yanked it back.

Maggie grunted. She grasped the joysticks tighter, as if she was grabbing a hold of the Bridge itself. She leaned forward, determined. There was nothing like the prospect of death to give you zeal.

The Bridge moved a little. It was like pulling a tractor out of the mud. Maggie had done that many times before, and she hated it with all her heart. It was what had made her leave the life of a farm in the first place. Her father refused the aid of technology, despite her pointing out that his own vehicles were technology too. The pace of advancement frightened him. He said something was being lost. He might even have been right, but a lot was being gained too. Maggie just wished she had something more to get the Bridge moving.

"Maggie," Larsman said over the comms.

"Yeah," she replied, her voice as strained as the tethers.

"We need those ships."

"I'm working on it."

It didn't help to see Larsman's worried face, so she tapped the viewscreen off, leaving just his worried voice. She could drown that out with her racing thoughts and fleeting breath. It was as if she was pulling that ship herself. There were so-called strongpeople who did just that, hauling entire starships across a docking bay, though she always thought they must've cheated with hidden boosters or hoverpads. She didn't have the luxury of cheating, maybe not even cheating death. The hull of the Offspring bulged like her straining muscles.

The Bridge moved a little more, metre by metre in the immeasurable vacuum of space. Each tug pulled it a little farther, its own momentum starting to help the process. Faster it went, two metres now, then three. All the while, another swarm of fighters approached at lightning speed.

"Come on!" Maggie urged, saying it out loud, an order to herself, a command to her vessel, a plea to the gods of metal and muscle, who found in her a new believer.

She could see the fighters fast approaching, those ominous blinking lights burning little marks in her mind. Then, just as the fighters came into view, and she gave one final tug before readying to release the cables and prepare for battle, Gemini Left cruised by, crashing straight into the oncoming swarm. The explosions came like a chain reaction, some from the fighters, some from the hull of the rocket itself. The remaining fighters turned their guns upon it, while its own guns came out rattling.

Maggie continued her monumental struggle, painfully aware that she might be able to have a bloodless battle, but not everyone else wanted one. Peace required the participation of all parties. Some people, for whatever reason, preferred war.

She hauled the Offspring to its docking position, letting it dangle. Normally an AAA would do the docking, guiding the vessel in gently. Instead, she tried to keep it roughly in place, while crew aboard either rocket fired magnetic tethers from either side and yanked it into place. When she got the go-ahead that it was docked, she loosed her own tethers and began the docking procedure for her own vessel. It was harder than she expected, and it took some time to line up properly, but there was no guesswork when it was done: the lighting aboard the ship changed from red to blue.

"Great work, Maggie," Larsman said.

She was about to respond, but he interrupted her.

"Now, buckle up. We're gonna go to warp."

The parts of starship Gemini had barely slotted together before Larsman powered up the Infinite engines. In the blink of an eye, the vessel slingshot across the galaxy, out of the reach of the swarm. The Infinite engines burned bright, connected together by the Bridge, creating energy out of nothing, and fuelling the massive thrusters at the rear of each rocket.

Inside, the warp stabilisers barely managed to keep everyone in place. Without them, the entire crew would have been thrown with such violent force that they would have been killed instantly. So much rested on the stabilisers that they were cordoned off from most of the crew, and given a permanent watch in Engineering on Gemini Right.

"We did it," Larsman said, his ugly mug showing up on Maggie's screen once more. She still clutched the joysticks, almost afraid to let them go. The ship shook violently as it thundered down the slipstream, travelling many times faster than light.

Maggie smiled. "We did it."

Then she thought of Skip, and her smile faded. Then she thought about where their journey would lead them, further out towards the Edge.

16
uncomfortable truths

In the dank, dark prison aboard the space barge, Skip had his own troubled thoughts. He didn't like where he was or that he'd been captured, but more than anything he didn't like what El-erae had told him.

"That can't be true," he said. "Humans have never been out this far."

"They have, though they never returned. But that doesn't matter. You sent your waste out here, drifting endlessly. In time, Sonata V's gravity pulled some of it in. Then you didn't just let it drift. You calculated flight plans to send it straight into our grasp. It wouldn't be so bad, except it was endless. Infinite waste. Our planet was swallowed up by it, one big dumping ground."

"Then how did your people survive?"

"That's why we can't complain too much," El-erae said, "or at all, really. It was your careless dumping that made us, especially your nuclear leftovers. The exposure made us mutate and evolve more rapidly than nature would have allowed, turning us from mere rats in the sewers to this, a race capable of getting up from all fours, of standing up, of reaching out to the very stars—maybe even to the planet that destroyed ours."

Skip scoffed. "So this is what, revenge?"

"I'm not sure what this is, human. We've come to terms with our conditions, with our quality of life, even with the short lifespan we live, which our scientists think is due to the radiation. But that is life for us. We have known no better. Indeed, we have known worse."

"So, what changed?"

El-erae's voice became hushed. She seemed hesitant to speak at all. "*They* came."

"Who?"

"You've never met them, have you?"

Something twigged in Skip's mind, something uncomfortable. It was buried, deep down, so he pushed the feeling back where it belonged.

El-erae shifted in place. "They go by many names. To us, they are the Yuuamaka, the Masters. They came and lifted our people up, out of the sewers. For generations, we thought they were gods. Some still do. They gave us ships so that we could travel up to heaven. They gave us this space barge, the Ark."

"This weapon," Skip said.

"So you know its purpose."

"I recognise a weapon when I see one."

"And its target?"

"Still working on that."

"I wouldn't take too long, human. You might find your home world gone by the time you figure it out."

"Alpha Prime?"

"If that's what you call it, then yes."

"But why? We're not at war with you."

"Not with us, but you never ended your war with them."

Skip shook his head. "With who?"

"I think you call them the Umbra. You don't yet call them Masters … but you will."

17
an uneasy
interview

On Gemini Left, Galaxy Express journalist Ted Nebula (presumed to not be his real name) was locked in Admiral Mendan's room with the renowned military man. He had just sat down for an interview before all this excitement kicked off, before the crew locked him inside for, they claimed, his own safety.

"What's happening now?" Ted asked when they initiated warp travel. He had never been on a ship that could travel as fast as this, and never one that was this far out beyond the known. It was simultaneously thrilling and terrifying.

"You've travelled faster than light before, lad, haven't you?" Mendan croaked. His voice was as frail as he was. He was more shrivelled up than the Ad Farans of the Jolda system, who had been crudely nicknamed the "space raisins" by others in the galaxy. The admiral could barely see, barely walk, need the help of an aut to get out of bed or bathe, and had to get his nutrients by hypershot. At one hundred and fifty-eight years old, he shouldn't just have been retired—he should have been dead. It seemed like it was the will of the Emperor alone that was keeping him alive. By rights, he shouldn't have even been flying. Ted had secretly been preparing a piece about how the admiral was being hauled around as a trophy hero of bygone wars, a way to bolster the Emperor's failing ratings. He knew it would get him in trouble with the Empire. They hired him to write a very different piece.

"Yeah," Ted said.

"Well, this is *faster* than faster than light. Didn't you do a piece on the Infinite engines?"

"That was my colleague."

Mendan grumbled. "They should have sent him."

Ted clutched his chair as the vessel periodically shook.

"Lad, you won't fall," Mendan said, picking at the few strands of white hair he had left. "We call that space turbulence. Even with our Dust Deflection Array, we hit some rough patches. They're microscopic, but they cause some trouble. It'd take you years to hit them if we weren't travelling at these speeds. It's the speed that makes it dangerous."

Ted gulped. "Dangerous," he said, biting his lip.

Mendan eyed him with not a hint of sympathy. "Take a shot if you've got space sickness."

"I'm fine."

"Well, get me one, will ya? I've always hated flying."

"An admiral that hates flying," Ted said as he collected a hypershot from a dispenser close to the door. He handed it to Mendan. "Imagine the headline."

"You won't be writing that," the admiral said,

taking the jab in his arm. He clenched what few teeth he had left. His dappled skin went a little pale—or rather, a little paler.

"Why's that?" Ted asked, making notes in his mind.

"Well, this is all off the record. A military manoeuvre."

"I wasn't given any—"

"It doesn't matter what you were given or weren't given, lad. You can put that datapad away, and you can turn your ocular implant off too. You won't be using any of that footage if you know what's good for you. You're not under civil law any more. Those were torpedoes fired, and turrets singing. You're under martial law now. We've got different rules."

"Journalists are neutral parties," Ted said. He was about to rattle off the Galactic Charter of the Fair and Free Press, but Mendan silenced him with his eyes. It made him wonder what the admiral could do with a gun.

"I've lived through many wars, lad. There's no such thing as neutral parties. You're on our ship, which means if we're boarded, you're just as much at risk of dying as the rest of us. So, if it comes to it, you'll take up a blaster and march out as if you were wearin' the uniform."

Ted didn't disagree or complain about that idea, at least not openly. He'd been on the front lines of some battles, mostly of uprisings on the dissatisfied planets in the Middle Ring. They were quashed easily, and with far more force than necessary. He'd been "advised" to document that level of violence as deserved by the rebels, as a warning to others. In it too was a warning to him.

"What do you think we're fighting?" Ted asked. He had his own answers to that. The Pan-Galactic Empire was over a thousand years old. It had grown big and unwieldy, spanning almost the entirety of the galaxy—so much so that they'd renamed the galaxy after it. Imperius. The old name was redacted from all the history books. The truth was out there somewhere, perhaps out beyond the Edge. That was what encouraged Ted to accept this job, despite the risk posed by the unknown. It was just a different kind of risk to that of living under Empire rules. Out here, outside the glance and grasp of the Empire, he could dig deeper. He was excited—and a little terrified—about what he might find.

"I *know* what we're fighting," the admiral said. He moved about uneasily on his seat. "I kept tellin' people they'd be back."

"Who? Who'd be back?"

Mendan leaned in close and whispered, "The Umbra."

18
savages

Skip would have liked to have learned more from El-erae, but their conversation was cut short by the arrival of As-hamaz, along with several other Raetuumaka similarly robed. These looked like the elders of their species, ones who had evolved intellectually beyond their fellows. They had developed immense powers of the mind, which they could exert on others, and so were called Mern-mazteles, the Mind-killers, in the Raetuum tongue. Even their mere presence was giving Skip a headache.

"Telling more lies, I expect," As-hamaz said to El-erae. She shimmied further into the shadows in the corner. Skip wasn't sure if she did it voluntarily.

"Hey," Skip said, drawing As-hamaz's attention. "I hope you brought dinner. I'm starving here. I mean, this isn't how you treat a guest."

"A guest?" As-hamaz said. His robes billowed as he laughed. "A man doomed to die."

"Well, what about a last meal, huh? What are ya, savages?"

As-hamaz didn't like that. Perhaps they had been dismissed as barbarians many times before. Perhaps he was attempting to rise above that, to elevate his species. If he was, he wasn't doing a very good job of it.

"Take him to the Way of Waters," he ordered.

His companions opened the cage door slowly. Skip lunged at them, but they did not defend themselves with their fists. They simply looked at him, and he felt a sudden pressure throughout his body, especially his head. He could barely move. It was like he was wading through a mire. A deafening ringing played in his ears, like some kind of sonic weapon. He was brought to his knees, exhausted, barely able to prod them with a finger, let alone a punch.

"All brash and brawn," As-hamaz said, though now he smiled. "Can't we settle our differences in a more … elevated way?"

Skip struggled up, shouldering one of the Raetuumaka away and reaching out for As-hamaz's throat. The sound began anew, crippling him, making his muscles like jelly, overwhelming his mind. He tried one last, desperate attempt to grab at his enemy, then collapsed to the floor.

"Why, Captain," As-hamaz said, "don't be such a savage."

19
the first death

They dragged him through many corridors and rooms, so many that it all passed in a blur to him. He wasn't sure if he was mumbling along the way or if their voices were mixed inside his mind. They seemed stronger than before, able to lift him with ease, though he half felt like he was kind of lifting himself. They brought him before an open hatch in the floor of a hexagonal room, dangling his head over the opening. It was dark below, so he couldn't tell how far the drop was.

"Your species," As-hamaz said, "is a disgrace."

Skip tried to shrug. "I know," he murmured. "What about it?"

As-hamaz snarled, then glanced at the others and blushed. He adjusted his robes awkwardly.

"You destroy worlds," he said solemnly. It kind of sounded like the start of a judgement. There was no trial. "This system was your testing grounds and your landfill. Sonata V, one great dumping ground for the so-called Pan-Galactic Empire. Sonata III, a husk from your nuclear weapon tests. Sonata II, with its quarantine shell, sealing off the results of your biological weapon experiments. You looked at our system, out here on the Edge, and thought nothing of the life here, so less 'evolved' than yours."

"I don't know what you're talking about."

"Of course not, Captain. Why think of us out here? The glory and wealth is to be found in the Alpha system at the Core of the galaxy. That is where the lie started as a seed. That is where the lie grows and festers, like a disease. If there was one world, or one system, that deserved to be wiped clean, it is that one. It is yours."

"Maybe so," Skip said, "but then aren't you just as bad as us?"

As-hamaz's temper flared again. He pushed Skip, who stumbled into the chasm. The fall was about ten feet, and he landed in a shallow pool of water with a splash.

"We will never be like you," As-hamaz roared down.

Skip struggled to his feet, almost slipping in place.

"Yeah," he shouted back. "We'll always be better."

"Mock us all you will, Captain. Now you face the First Death."

The hatch sealed tight, blocking out most of the light. Only a faint blade came through here and there throughout the passage, barely illuminating the curved metal walls. It didn't take much of an imagination—and Skip didn't have much of one—to think that it looked a bit like a sewers.

20
the way of waters

Skip wasn't sure which way to go. The tunnel seemed to go on endlessly in either direction. He didn't ponder it too long though. With nothing to go on, he decided to walk wherever he was facing. If the Raetuumaka weren't being kind to him, maybe the fates would be kinder.

He took a few steps, almost slipping again. He had to reach out to the walls on either side for support, taking each step more carefully. The water was a few inches deep at the bottom. It seemed to move constantly, almost like it had its own tide. Skip wondered what gravitational effect the ship had on it, and had on him. Even more, he wondered what effect those Mind-killers had, and how he could possibly fight them. He was built for wars of might and muscle, the Man of No Tears. He quickly buried the feeling that they might be the first to make him cry.

He followed the passage for a while, then halted as he thought he heard something. He turned around, glancing in both directions, straining his eyes against the darkness. It seemed he was alone. Normally, that was a good thing. It wasn't the first time he found himself wandering alone behind enemy lines. Yet now a part of him felt like maybe he could have done with an ally. He didn't let that thought play out for long. He killed that part of him and gave it a quick burial. He couldn't wait for a friend. He had to do this on his own.

He pressed on, until it seemed like maybe the First Death would be exhaustion or starvation. He could see the thin crack of a hatch door above him every hundred metres or so, but there seemed to be no other means of escape. He tried jumping up to one, but it was too high. He tried running up the curved wall, but his feet skidded off the surface and he came down with a bang.

So he sauntered on, a little more defeated with each attempt to escape. Maybe that was the intent, to whittle him down, to break him. The thought of it only made him more defiant.

He remembered his childhood on Alpha Prime, when the other kids said he couldn't cross the Energy Bars before the metal gave him a zap. They said he had rockarms, that his muscles were too weak from the lower gravity of his asteroid home. They taunted him, and he rose to the challenge. The bars defeated him time and time again. His fingers slipped, or the zap came before he could get across in time. He fell, grazing his knees, and they taunted him more. No matter how strained he felt outside, and how broken inside, he kept getting up, and swore to himself that he would not cry. Day after day he went back there. Some said he was seeking his punishment. He felt he was seeking his reward. He was searching for his ascent above the people who tried to drag him down—just like, perhaps, the Raetuumaka were.

Each day he grew a little stronger and got farther across before he fell. Then some of the Alphans, perhaps feeling threatened by his progress, started to throw rocks at him. "A rock for the Rockborn," they jeered. No matter how many bashes and bruises, he kept going. He wouldn't let go. As much as he clutched the Bars, he clutched this dream of his to make it to the other side. There, he would find his hidden glory, his way to climb above his station. There, he would find what it meant to be a man, and the strength to be a soldier.

When he finally made it across, the other children said he cheated, but he knew in his heart that he had won that victory through perseverance. From that day forth, whenever he felt that victory was far off, that the odds were too great, he reminded himself that all he had to do was put one hand before the other, that all he had to do was persevere.

21
the Ragged belt

Maggie had barely gotten up out of her seat when she saw the lights change again. They were slowed down to sub-light speed—already. As much as Cada had overclocked the engines, there was no way they had reached their destination this soon. That only meant bad news.

"What's up, Larsman?" she asked over the comms.

"Buckle up, Maggie. Asteroids ahead."

The Dust Deflection Array could obliterate the tiniest specks of dust in space, which at faster than light speeds would have otherwise torn the ship apart, but against larger obstacles like asteroids they didn't stand a chance. The impact would have been like setting off all the nuclear waste aboard the space barge they had just fled from. So they slowed to sub-light speeds, turning to manual manoeuvring, and began to separate the different parts of the ship to better traverse the asteroid field.

Maggie sat back down, taking the controls of the Bridge. Larsman boarded the Offspring, taking manual control there, while Toz separated the rockets from the fighters. The ship broke apart just in time for the first group of asteroids, which seemed to be travelling at great speeds. A few of the smaller ones struck the rockets, which took longer to turn, while Maggie and Larsman bobbed and weaved through the others.

The rockets fired off in either direction, attempting to go around the asteroid field, but the distance was vast. Yet, the chances of dodging the space rocks was small. They could have outrun them with the power of the Infinite engines, but the prospect of a high-speed impact was too much to risk.

Maggie watched as Larsman wound his way through the asteroids with ease, taking chances she wouldn't have dared to take. He dove straight towards two rocks that were about to smash into each other, narrowly clearing the gap before they crashed together. They bounced away, opening the path for Maggie to follow.

Gemini Left fired at some of the incoming rocks, breaking them apart or pushing them away. Gemini Right used its many shields to block some of the impacts. Meanwhile, Larsman dived and spun, and Maggie tried desperately to follow his ever-shifting movements.

Then Maggie thought she saw the colours on one of the asteroids change. She tried not to glance back, for fear she would miss a new obstacle on her path. Yet, even with both eyes ahead, she could see the shadow of something pass behind her. The computer picked it up too: a giant, worming creature, which had coiled itself into a ball, its cracked skin camouflaged to look like rock. It travelled with the asteroid field, hidden, waiting for some hapless prey to enter. Then it moved in for the kill.

"We've got company," Larsman said over the comms. He pulled up hard, skirting over the body of another of the space worms that awoke before him. Maggie turned right, just as the head of the first worm came by, jaws open. She zoomed through its open jaw, clipping the tip of one of its jagged teeth before it chomped down with a force that sent out a shockwave.

"Colony-eaters," Toz said. Maggie had heard of these before, though there were only three recorded attacks by the illusive creatures. They travelled usually in packs, taking a whole asteroid colony in their mouth before crushing and consuming it. Many scientists believed changes in space weather were causing them to travel farther into the galaxy, seeking new territory. Now the Gemini was in theirs.

"These are smaller than the reports," Larsman commented.

Maggie studied the awkward movements of the space worms, like the first wobbly steps of a child. "These are newborns," she surmised. "It's a nesting ground."

There was some relief in that assertion, for the fully grown forms could have swallowed the Gemini rockets in one gulp. Yet, it also made her think that somewhere out there was the mother or father, and if they came back to find their nest invaded, they'd be very angry.

Larsman had vanished out of sight, though his marker on the screen continued to move. Maggie only hoped it didn't move inside the belly of a beast.

But there was no time to worry about others. It was just as dangerous for herself.

The nearest worm coiled itself around a nearby asteroid—or perhaps it was another worm disguised—using it as a kind of springboard to launch itself towards Maggie's ship at greater speeds. She pulled up sharply, coasting along the ridges of its nose, if it was a nose, and then its eyes, and across the back of its neck and down its body. She turned quickly to avoid the lash of its tail at the end.

And there was the second worm, waiting for her, as if to snap the tail of its kin in the search for a meal. It was anyone's guess what these creatures normally ate, and if they were left out here to starve. Yet, whatever kind of compassion or mercy Maggie felt—and it was a lot—it was overcome by her own hunger to survive.

The creature wiggled its way towards her, swimming in the sea of space. Maggie's natural curiosity made her want to study it, to see how it moved through that great vacuum—indeed, how it survived out there, how it breathed, if it even had lungs. Yet if she watched too long, she would learn a different lesson altogether: how it fed.

She gave the thrusters everything, darting forward. She could almost feel the space worm behind her, diving between the asteroids that she passed through, flicking one away with the whip of its tail. Her speed was constant, which must have meant the worm was getting faster, because the computer's sensors went mad, telling her of an incoming "missile."

Then, just as suddenly, she found her ship engulfed in shadow, and looked out to see that she was in the jaws of the beast. She gasped audibly, so much so that her comrades heard her on the comms and feared the worst. In a moment of genius or madness—and likely a little bit of both—she killed the life support of her vessel, redirecting the power to the thrusters, which propelled her out of the worm's mouth a mere second before the jaws slammed shut.

She felt the sudden chill of the air, and then the increasing pressure, and then the suffocating lack of oxygen. She turned the life support back on, feeling the ship slow again. Maybe it was the reduced oxygen, but now she started to make more daring moves, ones that even Larsman would have hesitated to make. She drove straight for an asteroid, to the point that the computer warned of impact, and dove down sharply at the last moment, like one of the daredevil pilots in the Empire's Galactic Games. The worm came along behind her, swift and sudden, but its bulk made it harder to follow her final movement. The asteroid crashed into its body, sending it squirming away.

Maggie continued on, a little more confident now, having skimmed the surface of death and managed to pull away in time. Then several more asteroids ahead of her started to shudder. Many more space worms stirred from their slumber, awoken by the cry of their kin.

Maggie wasn't sure what to do. There were at least six of them blocking the path ahead. She thought maybe she hadn't cheated death at all—she had just delayed it. Maybe she wasn't destined to be the meal of one, but a feast split between an entire brood.

Then, behind the wall of rock and worm, she saw

Gemini Left pass by, with its many turrets turning into place. They opened fire, blasting through the gathering worms. The creatures roared out, perhaps a cry to their mother, before slithering away.

Maggie was never so glad to see guns blazing, and yet she felt a secret guilt that her life had been spared that way. She remembered Skip mocking her belief in the sanctity of all life, telling her that some day she would pick up a gun just like the rest of them. That day had not yet come, but many others were shooting for her. She didn't feel she could entirely absolve herself if the outcome was the same.

The asteroid field ended, and the pieces of the Gemini starship rejoined each other. They continued on at sub-light speeds, keen to get as far away from that nesting ground as possible. The fear of the mother returning was on all of their minds. They just hoped she wasn't coming back the way they were going.

They hadn't travelled far when they faced a new barrier. Ahead were a series of floating warning buoys, black octahedrons that periodically blinked red. They were different to the ones the Empire used, but their purpose was instantly clear. This was the literal rim of the Edge. After that point, the galaxy ended.

"Pull us back!" Toz shouted.

"We're safer out here," Larsman replied.

They drifted past the warning buoys, into the great expanse beyond the Edge. The Pan-Galactic Empire had no name for this region. It simply called it the Unknown. There were no records of humans having travelled out this far, and though Maggie was making some mental notes, she had a growing fear that she wouldn't live long enough to record them.

22
the rising tide

Skip kept walking, until his muscles began to weaken, and then he walked some more. Every step was harder than the last, and the water didn't make it any easier. Yet, no matter how far he'd have to go, he'd go there. He'd crawl if he had to.

As he went, he could hear footsteps far above, muted by the metal. A whole army walked above him, toiling away, readying their weapons, conspiring and colluding with whomever the illusive Masters were. He couldn't make out their words and could only imagine their deeds. It made him wonder what his own crew were saying and doing now. He couldn't hear them either.

Yet there were other sounds that were clearer in these sewers of the ship. The sound of creaking metal. The sound of gushing water. He added to them the splash of his boots in the shallows below him and the grunts and groans he made as he stumbled on.

Then he realised that the sounds he was focusing on were not a mere meditation for the march. They were things his gut was directing him to pay attention to. They were sounds that could save his life.

He reeled in his wits just enough to notice that

the water below him was rising. It'd been just below the lip of his boot, and now he felt the water seep inside. That must've been an inch higher than before.

Another valve creaked. The water flooded in more. He couldn't tell its source, only that it was rising steadily around him. Now he was waist deep, wading more than walking. The prospect of death gave him a second wind, but he thought he might need a third or fourth if he were to escape.

He pushed on, and the water pushed back. Its uncanny tide cast him back as many steps as he made, or thought he made. Those steps seemed easy when the tide moved the other way.

He looked up and around, searching for some exit, some little crack he might widen, some door he might unlock. He rarely looked down, where the water kept on rising. He didn't have to. He felt it slowly swallowing him. That it was slow was the torture of it all. In battle, death was often quick.

He struggled to kick off his heavy boots, and was only glad that he wasn't wearing his armour now. Yet, part of him wished he was. It had its own oxygen tank, and he might have been able to punch a hole through the wall with those giant gauntlets. The thought was no help to him now. It was like staring down the barrel of a gun and wishing you'd fired first.

He started to float, and swam up as high as he could, until his hands could almost touch the ceiling. He turned on the spot, looking for one of the hatches he couldn't reach before. It was so dark, he could barely see his own thrashing arms as he moved. Most streams offered the prospect of life, but this black river offered only death.

He swam on, feeling his way across the walls, and now the ceiling, catching his nails in the tiniest crack here and there, but finding he could do nothing to widen the gaps. His vision was blurring. The ebb and flow, and his own splashing, cast some of the dark water into his eyes, until he thought for a moment he'd gone under. It was no relief to find he hadn't, because the dread of it remained.

He thought he saw a faint light far off. He swam for it, ten metres, and yet the light seemed as far as ever. Maybe it was hope. He wondered if this was the point that most gave up, if they hadn't already. He saw their bobbing bodies in his mind, food for the rats. He swore that would never be him. He'd swim the even darker rivers of the Underworld if he had to. Part of him wondered if maybe he was already there.

He kept going. First it was foot after foot, step after step. Now it was arm after arm, just like it was as a child. He was made for this. The water taunted and jeered. He promised he would defy it, that he would overcome it, that he would ultimately triumph. Yet he wasn't a child. The tests of an adult had a higher price. Sometimes failure didn't just bring a lesson. It brought death. He had four decades under his belt, and wished he could cast them off to make him lighter.

He finally reached the source of light, finding a crack of about a centimetre between the doors of a hatch. He looked through it, and the light outside was blinding. He thought maybe that was a mercy, because then he couldn't see the rising waters. Yet his eyes adjusted, and he saw a boot pass by, and then a furry foot. He saw the shapes of Raetuumaka working away in the room above.

He thought about crying out for help, about begging for mercy. Maybe that was what they wanted. He wondered how many had gotten this far, past the bobbing bodies of their peers, and were left so broken that they auctioned their lives to the bidders above. They couldn't sell their souls, because by now they were shattered beyond repair.

He defied that urge inside him, just like he defied his captors. They could take all he had, but he wouldn't give it willingly. In that, they couldn't take his resolve. That was the one small victory he could take to the grave.

The grave was damp and rising.

He saw an eye suddenly appear at the crack. Someone had spotted him. There was a laugh above, followed by a series of shouts in the Raetuum tongue. He thought he heard As-hamaz's name called out. Then he saw the Mind-killer enter the room above and stand over the hatch doors, staring down. He smiled, and Skip had never seen so much glee upon the face of an enemy. Normally by now he had blasted it off.

"Seal it up," As-hamaz told the workers. He turned away, and with a clank the hatch doors sealed tight, plunging Skip into almost total darkness.

No, the light was not hope. It was just a veiled despair.

There was little left for Skip to do. The water caressed his throat, like a strangler's foreplay. It nudged his chin, forcing him to pull his head back, to take some final gasps. It swallowed his face, filling up his ears and nostrils, making a tributary down his throat. It had all of him now, all but the tips of his fingers, which still grazed the ceiling above. Then it had those too, and all that was left was the little victory of his resolve.

He blinked in the moving waters. He felt the suffocation. He thrashed involuntarily. Then the blackness faded to a different black, and all those racing thoughts reached the finish line, where it was altogether still.

23
some kind of afterlife

Skip had a vague recollection of being dragged out of the water and placed on a bed, of having his lungs pumped, of having his body filled with electrified needles. If that was what the angels did, he thought maybe he'd fare better with the devils.

When he awoke, he found himself back in the cell with El-erae, thinking his ordeal in the sewers was just a horrible dream. If it was, waking up wasn't a whole lot better. He feared he'd face it all again.

"One down," El-erae said.

"Huh?" Skip felt the grit in his throat. You'd think the water would have washed it down.

"The First Death."

"Stars."

"That'll come later."

"Death by stars?"

El-erae said nothing.

Skip shook his head, immediately regretting the movement. He felt like he'd been bashed with a thousand bats. Maybe that was another of the Dozen Deaths.

"So it was real," he said.

"Only as real as everything else," El-erae mused. The more Skip talked to her, the more he realised that she must have been some kind of Raetuumaka monk. Even her robes and the way she sat suggested this. It seemed like even when she talked, she was meditating.

"Everything's pretty damn real to me."

"Then you will feel the Dozen Deaths all the more."

"So they bring you to the brink."

"Oh, no. They bring you beyond."

"So, I really did die?"

"Yes, and they bring you back, before the final cord is cut. That is the ultimate torture, not allowing you to let go."

"What if you don't wanna let go?" Skip asked. He saw that childhood self, clutching the bars.

El-erae looked at him with eyes of pity. "Then the pain will be greater still."

Skip didn't want her pity, or anyone else's. He'd never gotten any before, and he didn't expect to get it now. If he got out of this mess, it'd be through his own efforts, not because someone just let him go. Maybe El-erae thought that made him his own jailer, but at least then freedom was within his grasp.

Skip groaned as he stood up. He never felt so sapped of energy before. He supposed he shouldn't complain. The dead didn't usually manage to stand up again.

He sauntered over to the cage door, resting against the bars. Perhaps they'd thought they had defeated him, that they'd won. Perhaps they, like the Alphan children, had gone home feeling victorious. He felt the overwhelming urge to prove them wrong.

"Well!" he shouted, as much as his weakened voice would allow. "Where's the next one?"

24
an unhappy second

The Gemini kept drifting slowly into the Unknown. Maggie sent Cada to fix the damage to the Offspring, while she rejoined Toz in the control room. She found her Second sitting in her chair, still gripping the arm rests tightly. He glanced up at her with fire in his eyes.

"Everything okay?" Maggie asked.

He scoffed. "Is everything okay? You've got some nerve."

"We made it."

"Barely. I'm sick of this, Maggie. I'm sick of following you to the brink. And by God, we're beyond the brink now! Why didn't you use your Executive Star to give me the reins? I would've kept us from crossing the Edge."

"I was a little busy," Maggie said. "Besides, Larsman's about the best pilot we've got."

"*They've* got."

"We can't think like that. Not any more. We're not two crew. We have to be one if we want to succeed out here."

"That's easy to say when they've got all the

firepower. There's no goddamn weapons on this side!"

"So?"

"Are you serious? Look at what we just faced!"

"Faced and won."

"Won? Our leader is gone, Maggie."

"Our leader? *I'm* your leader."

"Huh. I thought we were one crew? You were our leader once, Maggie, back when you weren't afraid to use a little force."

"You better watch your mouth, Toz. I'm not afraid to use it now."

"Send me over to Gemini Left and you won't have to hear me at all."

Maggie sighed. "I can't."

"You mean you won't."

"I don't have that authority."

"And you claim to be our leader?"

"They assigned you to Gemini Right, Toz. That was your punishment."

"We're out in the goddamn middle of nowhere, Maggie! They don't have any jurisdiction here. We don't even know who rules beyond the Edge. We could've just walked into a war. We've gotta be ready. We need fighting power."

"We can win this without weapons."

"I'm a sniper, woman! What good am I here?"

"You were useful before."

"Yeah, blowing through gates and doors. Do you think those explosives weren't weapons?"

Maggie had tried to forget those days. She had led her band of environmentalist rebels through the defences of Omega Prime, looking to expose what the Empire was doing there, and put a stop to it. It hadn't worked. This punishment was small compared to what happened to most. She knew it wasn't mercy. As soon as she and her crew stopped being useful, stopped sending back data and reports, and discoveries and experiments, they'd be made to disappear.

"At least we didn't hurt anyone," she said.

Toz laughed. "We didn't hurt anyone?"

"Well," she said. "At least we didn't kill anyone."

"Well, you know what, Maggie," Toz replied, prodding her in the should, "maybe we should've. If there were no witnesses, we wouldn't have ended up in this hell-hole."

25
the mad admiral

The crew of the starship Gemini were largely preoccupied with repairs, and catching their breath after the recent struggles. This meant Ted Nebula's attempts to free himself from Admiral Mendan's room fell on deaf ears.

"I guess we're stuck in here," Ted said.

"Bright as well as pretty," Mendan replied.

"Not sure about that."

"Yes," Mendan said. "Me neither."

"Shall we continue the interview then?"

"Is there any point?"

"It'll pass the time."

"We should be out *there*," the admiral said, strolling to the door to peer outside the glass. Crew members were running to and fro. "We should be preparing for the fight. You can bet your ass the Umbra have already prepared."

Ted bit his tongue. He'd heard that the admiral had gone a little wacky in his old age, but it was something else seeing it up close. Mendan had interrupted a live broadcast at the Pan-Galactic News Network to warn about the impending threat of the Umbra and had to be hauled off. It was an embarrassment for the

Empire. The admiral allegedly issued a statement afterwards saying it was an error, that he'd just had too much to drink (which was apparently a positive trait when it came to war heroes), but Ted didn't buy it. He had a feeling they'd ship him off somewhere far away, keep him out of trouble, and lo and behold, here he was—far away, but still making trouble.

"You don't believe me, do you?" Mendan said, sitting back down. "I didn't believe it either for a long time, until I saw it with my own eyes."

"Don't you have something like … what is it, glaucoma?"

"I'm not blind, boy! *They* did that to me. For all our science, our opticians said it was beyond their ability. We've had a programme of perfect vision in the military for the last two hundred years. No matter the ailment, we could fix it. No one was ruled out due to poor eyesight. The Empire would pay for it all."

"Not a bad exchange for sending you into war."

Mendan grumbled. "Yet this," he said, pointing to his eyes, which were now partially webbed over, "this is something beyond science."

"Nothing's beyond science."

"*They* are. I'm not even sure they come from this universe."

"The shadows," Ted said, finding it hard not to sound condescending. He couldn't write this. He was supposed to remind people of Mendan's past glories, help rekindle a sense of wonder in the Empire's achievements. He wasn't supposed to be writing ghost stories.

"Mock me all you want, boy."

"I'm not mocking you."

"I've tried for years to get people to believe me. Everyone thinks I'm crazy. I might have lost a lot in battle, but never my wits, never my mind. We defeated the Umbra a thousand years ago. Blast, who knows how we did it? Maybe they were weaker then. And in the mean time, we celebrated, while they regrouped. They learned. They adapted. They studied our weaknesses and silently prepared to strike. Now, we walked right into their preparation."

Ted didn't think the direction of their chat was going anywhere useful. The more Mendan talked about the Umbra, the more agitated he got, and the more Ted had difficulty stopping his eyes from rolling. He thought it better to change the topic entirely.

He glanced at the glass chamber in the corner, filled with water (or some other liquid), in which floated a woman's body. Her hair seemed to swim with a life of its own, but otherwise, she looked altogether dead. Ted had wondered if she was Mendan's wife, though she looked too young for him. He had heard rumours that it was his wife's death that started the descent into madness.

"I never asked," Ted said, rapping his knuckles off the glass. He instantly wondered if that was disrespectful, though he knew that the admiral would tell him quickly if it was.

"They *always* ask."

"Well, it's … a little odd."

"Like me, hmm?"

"I didn't say that."

"I bet you you'll write it though."

"This is off the record."

"Well," Mendan said. "Read the label."

"I did, but it doesn't explain what, or who, or … I don't know."

"That's the body of Glacia Andros, one of the finest soldiers I had."

"Why's she in the tub?"

"I'm gettin' to that, boy. Sheesh! No patience with your generation. As I was sayin', finest soldier I had."

"Finest or one of the finest?"

"What?"

"You said one of the finest first."

"Did I?"

Stars, Ted thought. *And he thinks he's still got his marbles?*

"No matter," Mendan said. "That's not the point."

"What is?"

"I was gettin' to it, I was! Where was I?"

"The finest soldier," Ted said.

"Right."

"Or one of."

Mendan growled beneath his breath. "I'll have you in that tub if you keep that up, boy. Do you want to hear this story or what?"

"Sorry. Go on."

"Right, so. She was there, leadin' Third Division, a hundred good men."

"All men?"

"Men and women. I call 'em men. Does it matter?"

"It matters for the facts."

"I thought this was off the record?"

"Oh. Yeah. Sorry. Force of habit."

"Y'know, a force of habit for me is shootin' people."

Ted kept his mouth shut then.

"Now," Mendan continued. "She was leadin' those men." He paused, eyeing Ted. "Those *soldiers*," he corrected. "And she was good at leadin' 'em. Got good fightin' out of 'em. Why, I could leave 'er to it. Didn't have to give commands." He sighed. "Though maybe I should've."

"What happened?"

"There was some kind of electrical storm. There often was on Trident Prime. We had to fly in between the *boltwaves*, as they called it. They were lightnin' waves. Never seen anything like it. They'd shoot across the ground, so they would, and then back, like the ebb an' flow o' the tide. Emperor knows how they worked. Might've been nature. Might've been something else.

"She said she saw something across the expanse. I told her to wait, but she'd gotten used to her own command. Got cocky, she did. If there's something I tell every young commander nowadays, it's: *Don't you dare get cocky!* We think we're smart, but the truth of it is that we don't know half of what's out there. Had a good lieutenant pull a gun on a *glasswalker* once, y'know. Reflected off and hit 'im right in the head. He thought guns worked on everything." He let out a long, audible sigh.

"So, she went in," Ted said. "Into the storm."

"By the Emperor's high collar, she did. Brought the whole Division."

"Then what?"

"We never heard from her again."

"Oh."

"We found her later, alone. We never found her men."

"Wow. I'm … uh … sorry."

"No point you bein' sorry, lad. She's the one who's sorry. Bet she regrets it now."

"Now?" Ted asked. "Y-y-you mean she's still alive?"

"Well, the scientists say she's dead, but I say different."

Ted stifled a sigh. She looked pretty dead to him. He sat back down, feeling like he was in a jar of his own, trapped and suffocating. This was supposed to be a quick job, a way to get some easy credits, and maybe crack open a new story—if the Empire didn't crack him open first. There was something about being trapped with a madman that put him on edge. Maybe it was the way Mendan told the story, or maybe it was how the light fell, or how the mind plays tricks, because when he looked at Glacia Andros in the glass chamber, it kind of seemed like she moved.

26
Suiting Up

After the encounter with Toz, Maggie went straight to her lab, where there were several half-abandoned projects, some that she was working on before this whole debacle began. One of them, in the corner, was an armour suit similar to the one Skip and his soldiers wore in battle, but heavily modified to suit Maggie's style of fighting: defensive. All the weaponry was replaced with shield generators and other means of survival. It wasn't quite finished, but then not many of her projects were. Even when she was working on it, she had a feeling Skip would put them in a situation where she'd need it soon.

Despite all the technological progress in the Empire, it was still a little backward in many other ways. Many men still saw her as incapable of command, and some of the crew aboard the Gemini were no exception. She still remembered when Larsman tried to make her "more appealing" to the crew by handing her some lipstick, which he said would go well with the bronze of her skin. If she were the violent sort, she would have made him swallow it. She wasn't. So, she used it to write equations on her mirror. Some of them were still there in vibrant red, a reminder of the logical course of action she so often took. To some, her current choice wouldn't seem logical at all, but she had thought it out. She had added up all the variables, including the element of surprise. She only hoped it would get the result she'd worked out in her head.

She gave the armour a once-over, checking for any damage it might have suffered in the hectic flight. Everything appeared to be in good order. She took it down and started suiting up. The weight of each piece was phenomenal, so much so that it was difficult to move when she had everything bar the helmet in place. She had added little boosters throughout the armour to help address the movability issue, but she hadn't had time to test them. Some situations didn't wait for the luxuries of the scientific process.

She was just about to put the helmet on when the door opened and Toz walked in.

"I knew I'd—what're you doing?"

"What's it look like I'm doing? Suiting up."

Toz shook his head. "Where're you going? There's nothing out here."

Maggie placed the helmet on, and anyone looking upon her wouldn't have known who it was. Her voice sounded stronger and more resonant through the mask.

"I'm going to rescue Skip."

27
Flying Solo

Before Toz could change her mind, she stepped into the transporter. She could hear the pad groan beneath the weight of her armour.

"This is madness, Maggie. This is exactly what Skip'd do."

"Right," she said. "We don't have to like each other, but we do have to work together. We're only as divided as we allow ourselves to be. He's one of us, so I've gotta do what I can." That was the funny thing about believing in the sanctity of all life—it included Skip.

She signalled for the transporter to bring her to the pad closest to the Bridge on Gemini Right and boarded the fighter-bomber.

"Unauthorised access," the computer said.

"Override."

"Override not permitted."

"Who's blocking access?"

"That information is not accessible."

"Override. Clearance: Maggie Aries Antwa. Code: Y2-68J7."

"Override not permitted. You do not have the necessary level of clearance."

"Damn it, what's happening here?"

That wasn't meant for the computer, but it answered anyway. "You are being refused access to the controls of this vessel."

"Only one person on this ship has higher clearance than me, and that's ... that's Skip. He's not here."

"Please state your request in the form of a question."

Larsman's image appeared on the viewscreen. "Howdy, soldier."

Maggie rolled her eyes. "I should've known."

"You're lookin' mighty fine today all suited up. Shoulda joined the navy."

"Looks like I didn't need to. I'm seeing enough battle as is."

"Maggie, we're formulating a plan to rescue Skip."

"Good. I can help."

"It doesn't involve you. Why don't you go back to the lab and grow some plants or something?"

"I'm more than just a scientist, Larsman."

"Sure thing, sweetheart, but why don't you leave the fighting to the real soldiers?"

"Because I don't see any on board."

"Maybe not on your side of the ship, but we've got plenty this side."

"I hear a lot of talking, Larsman. I don't see any action. That's the difference between you and Skip."

"Yeah, well, that's what got us into this mess in the first place, right?"

"Right," she said. "But we're here now. We need to act."

"When did you become all guns blazing?"

"The moment we lost one of our own."

"I thought you two hated each other?"

"We had our disagreements, but you know, out here, we're not that different."

"Oh, you and I *are*," Larsman said. "You're crazy and I'm not."

"I don't care, Larsman. How are you blocking my access? I have higher clearance than you."

"Yeah, but I have Skip's access card. He gave it to me before he left. Standard procedure. You might think you're in charge, honey, but even when Skip's not on board, he's still pulling the strings. He's the Captain, not you."

"And not you either," she said, turning off the viewscreen. She blocked the signal, one of the few things the computer would still let her do, and then ducked down beneath the console. The armour made it difficult to get down, and she could only imagine what it would be like getting back up. She punched through the casing, tearing off one of her gauntlets to pull at the wires. She hadn't hotwired a ship in quite a while. That was one of the things that got her landed with this galaxy service in the first place. She wondered if the galaxy would thank her for rescuing Skip, or if that story would be rewritten to make him out to be the hero.

The engines turned on and the security block ended. She struggled up and collapsed into the driver's seat, hearing the leather creak beneath her. She disengaged from the rockets and blasted off. Her eyes caught the flashing lights on the fighter console, highlighting the missing torpedoes. There hadn't been time to reload. That didn't matter. She planned to do this without firing a single shot.

28

a gamble

It took some time to get back to the space barge without the power of the Infinite engines. If Larsman had really wanted, he had could outrun her, even without the coupling of those engines. Each alone could outrun the Bridge at ease. But Larsman didn't want to go back to the space barge, at least not this soon. He'd made that very clear. Every second lost was one closer to Skip's death, if he wasn't dead already. Maggie didn't like the thought that she was potentially making this gamble for nothing.

She saw patrols of fighters circling the area. It would be hell to fight through them, and she had no fighting power. She was betting everything on defence. It had paid off before, but sooner or later the fates started favouring someone else.

She gave her boosters everything, thrusting the ship forward. Then she killed the engines and knocked off the lights. She let the vessel drift from its own momentum for a while, spinning a little, making it look like she had lost control. She assumed it must have looked good, because she felt she'd lost it too.

If she had told Larsman this plan, he would have locked her up with Admiral Mendan. Yet no one thought the same thing about Skip's mad ploys. More often than not he tripped and stumbled into victory than anything else. The Man of No Tears. The Man with No Plan, more like.

Maggie waited. For a while, it seemed like nothing was happening. Then the fighters spotted her, still drifting slowly towards them. They turned like rabid dogs who'd caught the scent. They didn't bare fangs. They bore cannons and turrets. Maggie didn't even have the shields up. By most accounts, this was suicide.

But Maggie didn't just fight her enemy. She studied them. She learned their methods, what made them tick. She'd seen how they reacted to the Offspring previously. They were scavengers first and fighters second. If there was no fight to be had, they would loot what they could. She was hoping for that. She was betting on it. Stars, a part of her that didn't even pray was praying for it.

The fighters approached, coming into firing distance. Maggie started to second-guess herself then. That was one of the big differences between her and Skip. She might have had her own impulses, but she was always questioning. Skip, on the other hand, just went with his gut, come hell or high water. Well, hell came and went, and the waters couldn't get much higher.

She sat back, waiting. She could see the targeting console showing that her vessel had been locked onto. They might have been scavengers, but they were cautious ones. They'd already learned what firepower the Gemini had. They weren't risking anything. She was risking everything.

They didn't fire. Two ships came in close, launching magnetic tow cables out towards her vessel. Then two more came and followed suit. In time, eight ships were there, hauling the Bridge towards the space barge, slow and steady. Several others flew alongside, an armed escort.

They pulled the fighter-bomber into a loading bay. It must have seemed like quite a catch. All of their vessels were makeshift, a mish-mash of different parts, a fleet of mismatching vessels. All of them looked stolen and scavenged. Yet they didn't have a vessel like this. Now they did.

The gamble was paying off, and all Maggie could do was sit back and wait it out. This part was treacherous, but it was still the easy part. As the vessel was pulled into place and a boarding crew prepared outside, she knew the hard part was just about to begin.

29
making room

Skip didn't make a good prisoner. He kept antagonising the guards, much to El-erae's dismay, though she had a way of talking that made it seem like she'd come to terms with everything, even him.

"Your actions will get us both killed," she said. She almost seemed fine with that. Her statement was more matter-of-fact than anything else.

"Maybe even a dozen times," Skip quipped.

He didn't joke so much when the guards opened the cell. He thought this was it. Death number two. It was funny, that. Humans usually only got one. It made Skip wonder if maybe cats chased rats because they had more lives than them.

The guards entered, and Skip involuntarily flinched. He wasn't sure why. He had trained for this. He had taken beating after beating and been tortured to death's door. He was ready for death. He just wasn't sure if he was ready for what was beyond.

But the guards passed him by and seized El-erae. He expected her to scream and fight, but she offered no resistance. Stars, they could have just asked her to escort herself out. She might have been at peace with it, but Skip was at war.

"Hey!" Skip shouted, but one of the guards kicked him back. Normally he would have grabbed that boot, twisted the leg, snapped the knee, and moved on to the next one. But now, after having died once, his reflexes weren't the same. He hoped it just required some time. He hated the idea that maybe part of him, the fighting part, hadn't come back with the rest of him.

They hauled El-erae outside, kicking and screaming, then slammed the gate shut.

El-erae's shouts diminished slowly as she was dragged away. Then the silence kicked in. That was when Skip could hear his own racing thoughts. It was also then when he saw a vast shadowy form, a billowing black smoke, creep down the corridor, passing by his cage. It almost seemed to turn and look at him, and he felt a horror beyond horrors. It continued on, down to where El-erae had been taken.

Skip tried to calm his breath. He'd learned techniques for that too, and they'd largely become second nature—except for now. He found the basics were becoming a struggle. His doctor had warned him about this at his last fitness test before taking position on Gemini. He gave him pills to counteract things. Those pills were in his armour, wherever they had taken that.

Skip tried not to think about the shadow, and tried not to flinch at his own. He suddenly felt like a child again, shaking as his father told him stories about the Umbra. *They'll get you if you don't go to sleep*, his father warned—as if that would help him slumber.

He listened out for El-erae's distant whimpers. It was silent. Maybe she was dead now. Maybe, after all, they only got one life. In place of her comforting presence and encouraging calm, he let his fears and paranoia build something else. He hadn't realised until now how much he was depending on El-erae, how she was keeping him sane.

30
last stop

Maggie waited for the boarding party. They didn't knock. They didn't ask her to open up. They took laser drills to the door, searing a hole in it.

Maggie stood on the other side in her full armour, ready to run.

They finished cutting, and the metal piece fell in with a clang. When they saw her, they were so off guard, they flinched. Some of them had seen an armoured foe like that before: Skip. Though they had defeated him, he had defeated many more of them in the process.

They pointed their guns, but Maggie didn't have any to point back. Instead, she hit the thrusters she'd built into her suit. They flung her forward, and she ran with them, half-galloping, half-propelled, darting right through the gathering guards. She knocked them over like bowling pins, shouldering some away, scaring away others with the sheer size of her armoured form.

She kept going, straight through the door they had come from, just as the first rounds of gunfire came her way. She slammed her wrists together, triggering the full automatic cycle of shielding. The energy shields kicked in all around her, knocking away the laser blasts.

She saw the route she'd mapped overlayed on her viewscreen. She had kept her scanners working almost silently on the ship as the Raetuumaka cut through. They were still working now, feeding her updates on the space barge, enhancing the scanners in her suit, which continued to map the route ahead. From that distance, they couldn't detect every corridor in the ship. She had to get closer.

She counted on one thing that counted against her before: the Raetuumaka would have their vitals dampeners on. Skip didn't have that technology. That meant the only life sign Maggie picked up had to be him. She was hoping the Raetuumaka wouldn't cop on to her plot and start randomly disabling their dampeners. This was already enough of a death trap as it was.

She continued her race through the corridors, bowling over any Raetuumaka in her way. The force of her strikes, enhanced by the boosters, knocked many out cold. A few that weren't quite unconscious played dead. Sometimes in the game of battle, that was the right way to play.

Finally, she picked up the vitals signal, but when she did, she halted. *That can't be right*, she thought. The signal was coming from behind her, closer to her own ship. She hoped against hope that it wasn't one of the Raetuumaka luring her into a trap. In her mind's eye, she visualised Skip having broken free from whatever cage they had him in, hobbling his way towards the ship. It would've been some irony for him to depart and unwittingly leave his rescuer behind.

She turned and charged back the way she came, taking a slight detour as her scanners calculated a faster (and safer) route. Then she saw the blinking dot start to head up the passage she had just come back from, so she was forced to double back again. For whatever reason, the Raetuumaka were nowhere to be found. She could have sworn she heard them chasing after her. She didn't think they'd give up that easily, but then she had very little to go on with this new species. If she survived this, she would fill up many datapads with her observations.

She chased after the fleeting dot, which seemed to be taking a similar route to the one the computer had mapped—not *to* the ship but away from it. Maggie wondered for a moment if they had tortured Skip, if he had finally cracked (completely) and was now just wandering in circles. As far as she was concerned, that could have pretty much summed up his life.

Then, as she caught up and turned a corner, she bumped right into him. Except, it wasn't him. It was Alex Primus, and she almost crushed him in the impact. He fell back to the floor, letting his blaster slip from his fingers.

"Alex!" Maggie blurted.

Alex gave a sheepish smile as he fumbled with the blaster.

"What in Nyron's name are you doing here?" she asked him, pulling him to his feet. She snatched the weapon from him. By the looks of it, he'd left the charge on for ages. It was half empty already.

"I … uh, I … I—"

"Right, we don't have time for that. I'm looking for Skip."

"I know. I … I thought I could help."

"But you're a royal," she said. She realised that sounded offensive, but the truth was that his job wasn't to help, or to do much of anything. He was a prop, another part of the Empire's grand scheme to appear unified. It was anything but.

"I'm *more* than that," Alex protested.

"Go back to the ship. You'll be safer there."

"I don't *want* to be safe. I want to be out here, on the front lines."

Maggie grabbed him by the arm and started to haul him back to the ship. He tried to fight her, but he was just a kid. Even without her armour, he wouldn't have had any luck stopping her. His feet skidded along as she dragged him away.

"I'm not a child!" he cried.

That was evident when she approached the docking bay. The bodies of Raetuumaka were strewn across the place. She'd knocked many over, but she hadn't killed them. There were scorch marks all over the room from stray blaster fire.

"What in—?" was all Maggie could manage. The scene stole her breath.

"I told you I could fight."

You never told me you could kill, she thought. Maybe this would have impressed Skip, and boy did Alex want to do that bad, but it made Maggie feel ill. So much wasted life. This kid was undoing everything she was trying to achieve there.

She tried to refocus, opening the doors of the Bridge and throwing him inside. He rolled on the ground, groaning like a child that had just receive a spanking. He might have deserved worse.

Maggie looked at the blaster in her hand. She wasn't sure what to do with it. If she gave it back to him, who knew what trouble he would cause? Yet, if she didn't, he might have wound up dead—and there'd be hell to pay with the Empire for that. He was one of Skip's guests, on Gemini Left's manifest, but right now none of that mattered. Maggie felt almost entirely responsible for him. Indeed, if she hadn't flown back there, he wouldn't be there either.

"Here," she said, casting the blaster inside. "It's not a toy." She closed the doors and locked them with an encrypted code. He banged at the glass as she walked away.

She thought she heard his muted words. "I know." And maybe he did.

That frightened her.

31
a small step

Maggie continued on through the seemingly never-ending corridors of the space barge, attempting to move as quietly as she could in a suit that clanged with every step. For a while, there were no more guards around. She wondered if they had all congregated around the Bridge, and if they had all died there.

She pressed on, until she saw the backs of two Raetuumaka guards, who chattered away to each other in their strange tongue, which was mostly guttural. She tried to calculate an alternative route, but there wasn't one. She was about to dart towards them when she saw the weapons they carried: foot-long electrified rods, or *electro-bludgeons*, the kind of weapons designed specifically for the bulky metal power armour of the Pan-Galactic Marines.

She stepped forward gently, unsure if her movement really did make so little noise or if the noise was just muffled by her helmet. She hoped to the high stars that the Raetuumaka were talking loudly, that they were so lost in their conversation that they wouldn't hear her. One turned to the other and cackled. Maggie could see the corner of its eye.

The talk continued, and she took another step.

This was a time when ranged weaponry would have come in handy. She knew Skip would have scolded her for her lack of wisdom in not having a weapon at least as a last resort, but she would have just rerouted the energy from a blaster to support one of the scanners or shields.

Skip had questioned her focus on shields almost the moment she had boarded the Gemini, when she stripped the weaponry from Gemini Right. Skip took those weapons willingly. He spent much of his time replacing the apparently "useless" elements of Gemini Left, like the medical bay, with a bigger arsenal. The arguments they had were endless. Then, one day, Skip stopped debating her. She wondered why, until Toz revealed that the Captain had secured a tape of her capture. It was a long video, because it wasn't a quick capture at all. It took government forces almost ten full hours to break through her defences. Skip didn't argue then. She almost thought she even saw a glint of admiration in his eyes. It was a pity it didn't last.

Maggie took another step. She barely noticed that she was holding her breath. This was just like sneaking into the Omega Alloys facility on the desert world of Omega Prime, where she was certain the Pan-Galactic Empire was testing world-destroying weapons. Her little band of activists from the EEE had to tip-toe their way through security. It was agonising. So was this.

She was almost on top of the Raetuumaka. She stretched her arm out, reaching for one of their shoulders, ready to inject a temporary paralysing agent built into a retracting needle in the knuckle of her gauntlet. She wasn't entirely sure it would work on these, so she clenched her left fist as well. Just because she didn't want to fight didn't mean she wouldn't if she had to.

The Raetuumaka continued their chat, but one of them swiped its tail behind it, lashing off the side of Maggie's leg. Everyone paused. The rat-men turned their heads slowly, their eyes widening as they saw Maggie standing there.

In the flurry that followed, Maggie jabbed the needle into the neck of the closest Raetuumak. The force of the blow sent it stumbling, and the drug worked quick, forcing it to the slump to the ground. The other Raetuumak swung its bat at her. She blocked it with her left forearm, but the electric shock travelled through her whole body. She had built in some absorption for shocks, mostly from her own equipment, but the voltage of the Raetuumaka weapons was high. She hobbled back, gasping for breath, almost toppling over from the jolt.

The Raetuumak checked its slumbering colleague. It must have believed it was dead, for it went into a terrible rage, turning to Maggie with fury in its eyes. It swiped and swatted the air with the electro-bludgeon. The weapon made a threatening buzz.

Maggie tried to regain her wits, shaking off the shock of the electric sting. Her heart rapped and her skin crawled. Her eyes were more alert than ever, taking in the sight of the advancing enemy, waving its weapon around madly.

She had just enough clarity of mind to ignite her shields as the rod came down at her face. The electricity dissipated into the energy shield. Then she struck back, launching her fist at the Raetuumak, dropping her shield just in time to press her arm through. The rat-man ducked, then swung again, catching her arm with the rod. Another jolt zapped through her body, sending her stumbling back into the wall. It came again, and she barely got the shields up in time. Each time the rod hit the energy wall, its electricity seemed to weaken, but it also weakened her shields. In some fights, stalemate was a good thing, but there was another kind of stalemate where both parties were dead.

Maggie kept the shields up this time, and the Raetuumak kept its rod held high, waiting for the opportunity to strike. They circled each other, challenging each other with their eyes, watching for a slight tell, for a sudden movement.

"Warning," the computer on her viewscreen said. "Power at fifty percent."

She had lost too much power too quickly. She couldn't afford much more of this. It would do no good to drag Skip from his cell with no shields left for the race back to the ship. She hadn't came as prepared as she was on Omega Prime, when she brought backup generators, and backup crew.

She watched as the electricity circulating around the Raetuumak's weapon started to flicker. They were running out of charge too. The rat-man caught her gaze and glanced down at the rod. That was when she pounced, pushing the Raetuumak with all her force. It fell, and she came down on top of it, struggling with its arms. It struck with the rod, and she yelped and spasmed, then pressed one of its arms down. It hit again, and she cried out louder and gritted her teeth through the surge. She punched it once in the face, almost knocking it out completely, before she jabbed the paralysing needle into its neck.

As the Raetuumak's limbs slumped to the ground, she panted and wheezed. The sweat from her forehead seeped into her eyes, giving its own little sting. She rolled off the creature, onto her back, regaining her breath, taking a moment to rest, to let her tense muscles relax. Yet, she knew she couldn't relax. She couldn't rest. So, she struggled to her feet, feeling weak. She took a step forward, grimacing. Then another, letting the air whistle through her clenched teeth. She walked like the wounded, knowing well that she was walking to the next battle.

32
Some Kind of Rescue

Maggie picked up a signal. A little green dot flashed in her visor, staying perfectly still. She hoped it was Skip, and assumed he must have been locked up, because he wasn't moving. Not moving wasn't good, but at least the vitals signal flashed—it meant he wasn't dead.

She followed the signal, ducking into an alcove just in time as a much larger Raetuumak, around eight feet tall, strolled by. She watched as it patrolled the corridors, with no weapon in hand. Its bulging muscles suggested it didn't need one. She made a mental note to describe it as a Marauder in her classification of this new species. It passed around a corner, and she continued on.

In time, she found the cell where Skip was being kept. She could see him from the distance, through the bars. He looked a little like he had almost given up.

Suddenly, another Raetuumak Marauder came around the corner close to Skip's cell. It glanced at the Captain, then continued its patrol, passing the place where Maggie hid. She waited, and, as predicted, another Marauder passed by, perhaps the first she saw. They were making a circuit of the area, with a gap of about fifteen seconds between each.

She weighed up her options. Fighting them didn't seem like a good idea. They towered over her, and likely outmatched her strength, even with the support of her armour. She had a feeling she'd have a hard time sending them to sleep, and wasn't sure the chemical was strong enough for them. She needed a different plan. She needed Skip's help.

She waited for a Marauder to pass, then cast a data orb across the floor towards the cage. It was meant to roll inside, but struck one of the bars instead. She never had a great aim, which was another reason she didn't carry a blaster. Skip perked up, glancing about. He couldn't see anyone, so he sunk his head again.

Maggie hid once more as another Marauder came by. She was glad it didn't notice the little steel bauble perched by the bars. She could hear its snorts as well as its heavy footfalls. She wondered if they were a natural subspecies of the other Raetuumaka or if they were genetically altered forms, enhanced with steroids like the Bulkers of the Pan-Galactic Marines.

She repeated the procedure, rolling another data orb towards Skip's cell. Again, it missed, striking the cage. He looked up, but didn't seem to notice the objects outside. Maggie wondered if he thought he was imagining things.

Another Marauder came around the corner, but this one caught the edge of the newest data orb with the tip of its toe, kicking it down the corridor. It bounced off the walls, back and forth. The Marauder jumped on the spot, launching into a fighting pose. It snarled and growled, looking around slowly with crazed eyes. It sniffed the air several times. Maggie was glad her suit disguised her scent. It passed on, slowly, making the ground tremor as it went.

Maggie peered out and saw Skip at the bars, reaching through. He had finally noticed the first orb there. She signalled to him before diving back into the alcove, where the shadows were her only ally. She waited for one more patrol, then gave another signal to Skip. She didn't know military signs, so she had to make it up on the spot. She waved her hands madly, hoping he got the idea that she wanted a distraction.

She hid and waited. Then she heard Skip shout, "Guard! You!"

She glanced out and saw the next Marauder turning and approaching Skip's cage. The Captain puffed his chest and rattled the bars. It seemed like he was looking for a fight. The Marauder slammed its fist against the bars. The echo continued for a while.

That was when Maggie charged out. She gave it her all, thundering down the corridor, well aware that the noise she made in the process would alert the Marauder before her. It turned, just in time for her lunge. She slammed it into the cage, but it immediately fought back, grasping her in a bear hug. Her armour groaned.

Skip reached through the bars, grabbing and punching. He tore a piece of fur off in his hand. The Marauder didn't even yelp. It focused all its energy and strength on Maggie, slowly crushing her armour.

She could hear parts of it pop and felt others buckle. A fuse sparked somewhere amongst the metal plates.

She could do nothing. Her arms were pinned against her chest. She couldn't turn on her shields, and that would have been useless anyway. The best she could do was stomp on the Marauder's foot with her heavy boot, but even that barely loosened its grip.

Skip continued his own struggle from the cage. He grabbed the creature's jaw and tried to snap its neck, but it resisted his strength. He bashed at it. He roared at it. Then he managed to reach his fingers further up, poking the Marauder in the eyes.

That was it. The creature howled, letting go of Maggie. It reached for its eyes, shaking off Skip's hands. Maggie reached for its throat, jabbing the knuckle needles of both hands in deep. It didn't even seem to notice at first, until the chemical kicked in. It froze, then toppled over, slamming into the ground.

"Stars," Skip said.

"Let's get you out," Maggie said, fumbling through the belongings of the Marauder in search for a key.

"Look out!" Skip shouted.

The next Marauder had come around the corner and spotted them. It charged, knocking Maggie over and pinning her to the ground. She struggled, but it was far stronger than her. It slammed her helmet against the ground. Her head smacked the screen inside.

Throughout the struggle, she vaguely noticed Skip pressed to the ground, stretching his right arm through the bars. He snatched at the belt of the fallen Marauder, rummaging through until he produced a key. He tried to unlock the cage, but it jammed. He thrust his shoulder against it. The cage shuddered. He tried again. The lock gave a little more. Again. It swung open with a clatter.

Maggie could do nothing but watch the scene unfold. She waited for Skip to throw himself at the beast, to jab at its eyes, to tear at its face. Instead, he ran. She was so taken aback by it, she wasn't sure what had happened. Skip ran down the corridor she had come from. He just … fled.

And then he came back, brandishing an electro-bludgeon. She watched as he fiddled with the controls on it, turning the electrical charge up to its highest setting. The rod almost exploded with energy. Then he swung it at the creature. It screamed and writhed, rolling onto its back. Skip kept going, digging the rod in, giving a cry of his own as the Marauder's fur began to cinder. It convulsed for a moment, then fell still and silent, as the smoke rose from its body.

Skip helped Maggie up.

"Damn, Skip," she said. "You didn't have to kill it!"

He shrugged. "Oh, yeah, I did."

To any watching, it seemed that maybe they would have an argument about that right then and there. They seemed so diametrically opposed, but deep down they were two sides of the same coin. He was sword and she was shield. Separate, they were both vulnerable. Together, if they could ever find a way to really work with each other, they would be powerful beyond measure.

Another Marauder appeared. It halted and

bellowed out. Two more came racing towards it. The three of them looked at Maggie and Skip standing over their two fallen comrades. Together, they gave the most ear-rending roar.

"I think we better run," Maggie said.

And, maybe for the first time ever, Skip said, "I think you're right."

33
batten down the hatches

They ran. Skip waved the electro-bludgeon behind him as they went, warding off the pursuing Raetuumaka Marauders.

"Quick! In here," Maggie said, racing into a storage room. Her sensors scanned the crates and boxes, which mostly seemed to contain food. There wasn't a weapon around. Maggie felt on two minds about that.

Skip followed her in, and the duo immediately barricaded the door, dragging some of the crates over and stacking them high. Maggie had to do a lot of the heavy lifting, thanks to the enhanced strength of her power suit. She could tell that Skip felt emasculated by it. The last thing she needed was for him to try something daring, to show just how macho he really was.

The door shuddered as the Marauders banged against it.

Skip sat with Maggie with their backs against the crates, shoving them back into place whenever the straining door moved them out a little.

"Well," Skip said.

"Well."

"A fine mess you got us into," the Captain said.

"*Me?* You're the one who got caught."

"I had it under control."

"Sure you did."

"I did."

They looked at each other, continuing the battle with their eyes.

"I had it all mapped out, Mags," Skip said. "I was gonna get them to take me to their leader."

"And then?"

"And then I was gonna kill him."

"Right."

"So, you see, you've kind of ruined my plan."

Maggie rolled her eyes. "You're welcome."

Another thud against the door.

"I do appreciate you coming out here though," Skip said. He said it softly, as if he didn't really want it to be heard.

"It was nothing," Maggie lied. It was anything but.

"Still though."

They looked at each other, and this time there was no battle in their eyes.

"You're part of the crew," Maggie said.

"Which one?"

"Yours. Both. Ours." She paused. "I'm starting to think we might only survive out here by working together."

"Yeah." Skip looked away. "Sure, I've worked with worse."

"Pff. Thanks."

The door rocked once more.

"These creatures," Skip said. "Raetuumaka."

"What about them?"

"They seem to be under some kinda spell."

"I hope you don't mean that literally."

"I don't, but then … maybe I do. They're ruled by some other race which they call the Masters. I think we have to defeat them."

"I think our priority is on getting out of here."

"But we have to defeat them too. I now know where this vessel is heading. Alpha Prime."

Maggie didn't know what to say.

"It's a weapon," Skip continued, "disguised as a transport vessel. It's not just carrying waste, Mags. It's on a collision course. Try and shoot it down, and, well … you blow it all up, including you."

"So we need a way to disable it," Maggie said.

"Yeah. I'm thinking those Masters are probably the way."

"What if they're not?"

"Well," Skip said. "I'd kind of like to kill them anyway."

Maggie smiled. "There's the old Skip."

"He never went away."

"We might need him to get out of here."

Suddenly there were shouts outside. It was a familiar voice.

Maggie sighed.

"Who's that?" Skip asked.

"That's … that's Alex."

34
a Royal thorn

It was clear that Alex hadn't obeyed Maggie's commands. It was clear that he had broken out and followed her. And, by the sounds of his shouts, it was clear that he needed help.

Skip and Maggie glanced at each other, rolled their eyes in unison, and started pulling the crates away again. They seemed a little heavier this time, weighed down by their worries as well. They heard blaster fire, which only made them pull away the crates even faster, tearing the lid off one and casting it, and its contents, to the floor. They tried to open the doors, but it jammed halfway.

Skip leapt through the gap, spinning his electro-bludgeon, which caught the attention of one of the Marauders. The other two were closing in on Alex. One of them limped from blaster wounds. By the time Maggie squeezed out into the hallway, Alex was out of charge, and the Marauders were about to pounce.

She grabbed a *shieldwall* bomb from her belt and launched it down to where Alex was standing. Its tiny sensors detected the walls and fired out rays from either side. Once they hit the walls, a shield formed beneath them, blocking the Marauders' advance. She sent another down behind them, blocking them on either side. They banged against the barriers, making them shimmer. They wouldn't last for long.

Skip danced with his own attacker, taking one step in to jab at it, before stepping back to avoid its swipe. They circled, moving back and forward, striking and dodging. Then the Marauder moved in quick, trying to grab Skip in a bear hug. He ducked out of those bulging arms and lashed its ankle with the electrified rod. The Marauder hopped and yelped, and its uneven structure made it topple over with ease. Just as he was about to finish it off, Maggie charged in, swatting away his arm.

"No more killing," she said, before jabbing the Marauder with the paralysing needles.

Skip shook his head. "Where's the fun in that?"

"You should see what that mentality has made in Alex."

They looked to Alex now, finding him ducked down behind one of the glowing barriers, as if cowering from the Marauders trapped between the shieldwalls. Yet, on further inspection, he wasn't cowering at all. He had torn open a terminal on the wall and was rerouting some of the power to his blaster, replenishing its charge.

"He's an innovative one," Skip said, "like you."

"Not like me," she replied.

They approached the first barrier, where the Marauders bashed and roared.

Skip shook his head at Alex. "What're you doing here, boy?"

Alex grimaced at the last word. If Maggie had

said it, he would have told her he wasn't a boy, but you didn't say that to the Man of No Tears. You didn't complain. You wiped your nose and dried your eyes and kept on marching. That was the only way to make it as a soldier. Yet, no matter what he tried, he would never be one. The royals were there to sit and look pretty, to help prop up the Emperor.

"He doesn't want to be safe, apparently," Maggie said, rolling her eyes.

Skip blinked. "Huh?"

"His words."

Skip shook his head. "Don't even explain. Let's just get out of here." He tapped the first shield, watching the snarling face of the Marauder behind it. "Let's leave these fellows inside their playpen. Alex, you'll need to find a way around."

"Are you kidding?" Maggie asked. "We can't let him wander off on his own."

"I'm not a child," Alex said.

Skip gestured to the teen. "See? He's not a child. Besides, he has a blaster. And by the looks of things, he'll have an infinite charge for it too."

"I can fight them," Alex insisted. He held his blaster with grim determination. Maggie didn't mind the determination. It was the grim part that worried her.

The shields began to weaken from the Marauders' blows.

"Come on," Skip said. "Let's circle around this block and meet at the far end."

Before Maggie could protest, both Alex and Skip left, departing in opposite directions. Her scanner suggested they should meet up again in a few minutes, assuming there was nothing blocking their paths. That was an assumption she was very hesitant to make.

35
how they fall

Maggie continued on, following Skip around, until they saw Alex on the far end of a different kind of corridor, which was just a thin mesh bridge down the middle, with dropped to a lower level on either side. Alex waved his gun from across the way.

"See?" Skip said to Maggie. "Easy as target practice."

Maggie never was much good at that. She didn't like the idea that they were someone else's target practice too.

Maggie beckoned for Alex to cross the bridge.

He shook his head and pointed down a passage on his side. "I think this is the way out."

"It's not," Maggie said. Her scanners made that clear.

Then Skip dashed across the bridge, shouting. Maggie looked to see several Marauders approaching Alex. Skip leapt and kicked at the nearest, only for it to grab him by the leg and toss him aside, almost knocking the electro-bludgeon from his hand. Alex unleashed a hell-storm of blaster fire, while Maggie charged along the bridge.

Maggie dove into one of the attackers, wrestling

it to the ground. It fought back, twisting around her body, grabbing her in a headlock. If that had been her head and not her helmet, it would have crushed her neck in seconds. Instead, the power armour groaned from the pressure, like a submarine at the farthest ocean depths.

Despite the resistance, the armour started to buckle. Parts of her shield array splintered under the awful weight of the Marauder. She tried to trigger the shields, but they wouldn't work at this proximity. She'd built that in as a safeguard to protect nearby allies, but it worked just as good for enemies too. It seemed that her suit was simultaneously saving and killing her.

She saw Alex kill one of the Marauders, wearing it down with blaster fire. It tried to continue on its knees, then drag itself along on its arm, but fell limp at Alex's feet. Skip killed another with his electro-bludgeon, then moved on to hers, striking it in the back. She was never so glad of violence before, because the strike loosened its grip on her.

Skip struck again, and this time the Marauder picked Maggie up and flung her at the far wall, across the gap in the mesh floor. She struck and fell, down to the next level, which was at least twelve feet of a drop. She was glad she'd put responsive air cushioning in the suit for big impacts and falls. They helped soften the blow.

Then something else fell down after her, landing with a clatter. It was the Marauder, still smoking from Skip's attack.

Maggie groaned as she sat up. No matter how

much cushioning she had, it still hurt. If you were dropped high enough onto a pile of feathers, those feathers would have felt like jagged rocks.

"I'm coming down," Skip said. It seemed that all the attackers had been dealt with, and there was a hint of disappointment in the Captain's voice, as if he was just getting into the swing of things. She was sure there'd be plenty more for him to swing at.

"I'm fine," Maggie replied. "My scanners show me a way out. There's a lift on the far end. I'll meet you there."

She heard them race off as she struggled to her feet. Then the overlay on her screen started to go fuzzy, and blinked out entirely.

"That's odd," she said. She tapped her helmet.

Something drew her attention from the far end of the passage, where the shadows seemed to gather. She couldn't see anything, and her scanners were not picking up anything either, yet she felt a presence there—an evil one. With a scientific mind like hers, she didn't scare easily, not even after watching the scariest of movies. She didn't jump at shapes on the walls. She didn't start at unfamiliar sounds. But now, she felt an immense terror. Her breathing changed. The hairs on the back of her neck stood on end.

"Wait!" she cried. "There's … there's something down here."

She glanced up, but Skip and Alex were gone. No doubt they were waiting for her further on. Yet, she felt there was something else waiting for her on this level.

36
out of the shadows

It emerged. A shadowy figure came forth, the black smoke of its form billowing around it. It had no distinct shape, just a nebulous gathering of darkness. There was a sense of a deeper, darker part of it pulsing inside, like the core of a planet, or the maw of a black hole.

"Guys," Maggie said, taking one step back.

The shadow stepped forward. It half-floated, half-clung to the ground. The wisps of shadow that flowed around it grazed the walls, like the antennae of an insect feeling its way towards its prey. There were no discernible features, no arms or legs, no face. Yet it seemed intelligent, and it felt malevolent.

Maggie took another step back, holding her hand out in front of her, as if that could keep the shadow at bay. She had no idea what to do. It seemed like the kind of force that could seep through vents, that would not be blocked by doors, and maybe not even by shields.

The creature, if it was a creature, advanced to match her pace. As much as she studied it, it seemed to study her, though it exerted a feeling of glee to match her terror. Perhaps she had fallen into its lair or nest. Perhaps this was the result of all the radioactive material aboard the vessel, or some imprisoned fiend the Raetuumaka had acquired. Yet the words of Skip came back to her, and she wondered most of all if this was one of the Masters.

"Stay back," she said, though she did not know if it talked, if it understood her words.

It didn't stay back. It kept coming, moving a little quicker now, surpassing her pace.

"I mean it," she added, and she really did, but she had no threat to back it up. Perhaps she really meant to beg, to plead, to bargain with her life, to offer up the location of Skip and Alex, to promise surrender and servitude. All of those thoughts passed through her mind, as if it too had been clouded in shadow.

She backed away faster now, two steps, then three. The shadow glided along in pursuit.

"What do you want?" she asked. A part of her thought that maybe she could reason with it, come to some kind of truce. A bigger part knew that it had no interest in diplomacy. It was here to consume and command. It knew it could not command her, so that left only one option.

Then suddenly the shadow knitted together into a form like a human, though a shimmering form, with a stray wisp of darkness here and there. Maggie wasn't sure if it really was shadow or smoke, or some gaseous form. She had previously observed the gaseous species known as the Aethera during their last centennial migratory event. This, however, seemed to be able to control its form, to structure it in a way to match the species it encountered.

"We want peace," the creature said. Its voice was a booming, wallowing sound, and its form vibrated as it spoke. It was almost like it created the words by shaking its body violently.

The word *peace* had an effect on Maggie like the word *war* had on Skip. She let her guard down. She halted, willing to hear it out, to see what it wanted, to try to understand it, so that maybe, just maybe, they could find a solution.

The shimmering, now humanoid, figure approached, offering her its hand, which was a vague amalgamation of shadowy fingers, like a sculpture gone wrong.

"Total peace," it said, stepping closer, almost within grasp.

Maggie was about to reach her own gauntleted hand out, when it added: "Through total annihilation."

37
the longest flight

Maggie yanked her hand back in time. The sudden movement caused the shadowy form to burst back out into its more amorphous shape. The force of the burst made the wisps around the edge turn sharp like blades, before they faded into the dark haze.

Maggie turned and fled. She activated all the boosters in her suit, so she was thrown forward with every racing step. If it weren't for those boosters, the chasing shadow would have likely caught her before she reached the lift.

She slammed the lift door shut, but the shadow seeped through the cracks beneath. She stomped at it, but the touch was like ice, even through the armour. She hammered her fist at the lift controls, not caring where it brought her, so long as it was away from there. It rose up, slicing through the shadow that had crept inside, leaving little bits of it to shrivel up and fade away.

She pulled the emergency lever as soon as she got to the next level. She forced open the door, almost tripping as she leapt outside. She looked in both directions, panting, waiting for some other shadow to tear itself from the walls. She saw Skip and Alex running towards her, waving. As soon as they reached her, she grabbed their arms and pulled them with her as she fled.

"What's wrong?" Skip asked.

"Don't ask, just run!"

They had barely turned the next corner before they were faced with the shadowy form, its wispy ends billowing more rapidly than before, as if it was angry. The trio halted.

"Stars," Skip said. "Y-y-you see that too, right?"

"Yes," Maggie replied.

Alex nodded, but said nothing.

Skip's breathing was shallow. "I think that's ... I think that's an Umbra."

"The Masters," Maggie said.

Skip clenched his fists, activating the electro-bludgeon. "They're not my masters."

He raced towards the creature, despite Maggie's attempt to stop him. He swung, and the rod buzzed through the air. Then part of the shadow seemed to leap out towards the electricity and swallow it, like some kind of mouth. The entire charge of the weapon was consumed, and Skip was just glad his hand didn't go with it.

"Right, let's run!" he cried, belting off before the others. It was easier to run like your life depended on it when it really did.

The Umbra pursued them, seeming to run as much across the walls and ceiling as the floor. Its form was constantly shifting, becoming longer here, thinner there. It bulged in places and seemed to dissipate in others, as if it was losing limbs and growing new ones. It was anyone's guess what was really happening. The history of the Umbra had been occluded with myth. Yet now Skip and Maggie wondered if maybe those tales weren't myths at all.

Though Skip initially led the way, Maggie quickly took the lead, enhanced by her boosters. She grabbed the others under either arm as she passed, then fired up the boosters again. All three of them were catapulted down the corridor.

They turned into the next passage, finding a force of Raetuumaka waiting for them, some with guns, some with blades, some with electro-bludgeons. On any other occasion, the trio might have turned and tried to find another way, but they leapt into the arms of the army facing them—not with glee, but with less fear than of that which followed.

Maggie kept her clutch on Skip and Alex, though she felt them slipping. More than anything, it seemed that the young royal was fighting against her grip. Even Skip, as proud as he was, didn't feign bravado at that moment, but then he had learned long before that the fire well and truly burns. Alex was fresh to the fears that others had long let fester inside them.

Maggie's voice controls were busted from the earlier Marauder attack, and her hands were more than full. She had to use her elbows to activate the boosters again. The force of them flung the trio right into and through the horde of Raetuumaka ahead, bowling some of them over, while others leapt out of the way. She took a step here and there between each push of the boosters, dancing between the piling bodies of her foe.

Then she felt Alex slip. She tried to grab him, to hold him tighter, even to yank him along behind her if she could. But he fell. He tumbled into the pile of Raetuumaka, while the boosters continued to throw Maggie and Skip farther down the corridor, halting at the end.

Then she heard the rat-men scream, and those howls were horrifying. She glanced back, letting go of Skip, thinking Alex had started his slaughter, but saw that the Umbra was passing through the army. It seemed to consume each of the Raetuumaka as it passed, sucking them up into its shadow, then piercing their entire body with what looked like a thousand black needles. Then it gulped them up, seeming to consume them in their entirety. It broke them down into nothing, until all that was left was the shadow.

Alex sat up, looking about for his weapon. The Raetuumaka cowered and prayed around him. Perhaps they begged for mercy in their tongue, promising to do better, to work harder on the weapons, to do more for the Masters. They were each gobbled up in turn.

Maggie took a step towards Alex, but Skip grabbed her arm and pulled her back. The distance was greater on this side than on the side of the shadow. Even with the boosters, the Umbra would reach Alex first.

The teen gasped as he saw the shadow approach, then turned to look at Maggie and Skip. Maggie tried to run forward again, but once more Skip held her back. Then the shadow picked Alex up, and he cried out, before his body was pierced by shadow, and it swallowed him whole.

"Come on!" Skip shouted, dragging Maggie around the corner. It took a moment for her wits to return, and they returned more than a little frayed. She ran alongside Skip, following the route her sensors displayed. The image flickered on and off as the Umbra pursued. She was now moving on automatic. If the visor wasn't telling her the way, she would have run wherever Skip ran, or she might have run in circles—back to the consuming shadow.

They bulldozed their way through the fleeing guards. No matter where the patrols where, they had heard the blood-curdling cries of their comrades, and didn't trust in pleading or prayer. The only safety was in running. Skip and Maggie were proof of that.

They reached the landing bay, where the fighter-bomber waited. Skip's eyes widened at the sight of all the slain guards around the room. Maggie knew he thought she did it, but right now she couldn't bring herself to correct him. She couldn't even mention Alex's name.

They boarded the ship and Skip took the controls. Maggie pulled off her helmet and collapsed into the seat beside him. She stared at the viewscreen as he started up and pulled out of the hangar. There was no shield up around the Ark. The Raetuumaka saw no threat from space. The real monster was inside their ship.

38
PROCESSING

Skip flew the Bridge away from the Ark, reversing its last flight course, sending it back out into the Unknown. He looked at Maggie every now and then, appearing like he was going to say something, then stopping himself half-way through.

"You can talk," she said, when he did it for the tenth time.

"I was just … I was gonna say." He stopped himself and sighed. "You did everything you could."

Maggie was silent.

"Sometimes it's the luck of the draw," Skip said. "You can't save them all."

Maybe that was true, and maybe Skip had come to terms with that a long time before. He was a soldier, a general. He led people into battle all the time, knowing well some of them weren't coming back. He even sent some to battle in forces he wasn't allowed to lead personally, deemed too dangerous. The Empire didn't want to risk their celebrity war hero.

For Maggie, it was different. The only battle she had really fought before was on Omega Prime, which was only a battle because of her endless array of shields. She could have surrendered, but surrender meant death in the Empire. The shields were to ensure the safety of her team. The stalemate helped her secure a deal with the Empire negotiator, to ensure all her people got out in one piece. Sure, some of them would end up out here, or on other God-forsaken research facilities in the middle of nowhere, but at least they were alive. That was the one thing she prided herself on throughout all of this. The preservation of life.

"It's not your fault," Skip said.

She wasn't so sure about that. She brought Alex there, even if she didn't know it. She gave him back his weapon. She used the supposedly unbreakable encryption that the teen was able to hack. And, more than anything, she let him go. Part of her wondered if maybe she did it on purpose, if her old hatred of the royals and everything they stood for manifested in that moment.

"I hate to say it," Skip continued, "but … it happens. Stars, it happens all the time. It could've been one of us."

"But it wasn't," Maggie said.

"You'll get over it," Skip said with reassuring certainty.

Or, she thought, maybe she would end up like him, a little cracked.

"The only thing I'm concerned about," Skip said, "is how the royals will react." He paused, staring at the viewscreen. "But then, we might never make it back to the Core Worlds."

Maybe that was meant to be reassuring too.

"You know, we have to go back there," he said.

Maggie glanced at him, but said nothing.

"We have to go back and kill that thing."

And, perhaps for the first time in her life, the thought of killing something didn't upset her at all.

39
better late than never

It took only a minute for Ontri to board the Ark, but it took far longer than originally predicted to find his way around the ship. There was something about Skip's last overclocking request that had damaged his sensors, and also damaged his ability to detect faults. He followed the misleading directions for what seemed like hours, strolling through the vessel largely undetected.

For the most part, Ontri was left alone, but then he did find himself on parts of the ship that seemed largely deserted. What his sensors had suggested was a vitals signal turned out to be a heat signature from overheating sections of the space barge's vast engine. He hadn't seen an engine quite like it. It seemed to be powered by the same nuclear waste that was being loaded into weapons all across the vessel, and it spanned the entire length of the ship. Indeed, by Ontri's assessment—which might have been a little faulty too—more than half the gigantic size of the barge was made up of the machinery to get it moving. It clearly was designed to travel great distances, though it lacked the speed and efficiency of the Infinite engines. Ontri's conclusion was that these Raetuumaka, whom he had tagged as a scavenging species, should probably scavenge those engines off the Gemini. He wondered if the good Captain would be obliging.

Ontri wandered back and forth on the lower levels for quite a bit, coming back several times to what evidently appeared to be the same overheated sections of the engine. He made various assessments, ending with pondering if the good Captain would be obliging.

The loop only ended when it was broken by the intervention of an outside force. One of the Raetuumaka engineers stumbled into Ontri, dropping all his tools in surprise. "Who ... what ... are you?" it asked in Raetuum. It seemed that they had scavenged so much, including many auts, that it wasn't sure if it was part of the hoard.

Ontri smiled. He always did like being asked about himself. He assumed it was a very human thing. "I am an invader," he said pleasantly, almost beaming with pride. He hadn't tried invading before. It was a new skill, and he did very much like learning and implementing new skills.

The Raetuumak looked dumbfounded. He kept glancing down to his tools.

"Do you need some help?" Ontri asked, bending down to pick up some of the implements. By the time he straightened up again, the Raetuumak engineer was gone. His assessment of the general air of the creature was: panicked.

"How very strange," Ontri told himself. He made a mental note to try running away from someone while they were not looking. He presumed that feeling panicked might be a natural prerequisite to making that work effectively.

Now that the loop was broken, Ontri started to wander upstairs. He found himself overhearing conversations in the Raetuum tongue, and quickly building a database of the language. He had a more sophisticated version of the auto-translator that all crew members had implanted into their ears. He felt a lot of things made him a little bit human, but he supposed those chips made them a little bit aut.

Knowing the Raetuum language proved immediately useful, not just for eavesdropping on the guards and thus avoiding most of their patrols, but for reading signs on doors and walls. He followed a lost engineer to a map console, which had the entire layout of the ship. The Raetuumak eyed him suspiciously, but Ontri made a comment in Raetuum about the lovely space weather, which seemed to help.

Once the console was free, he started to hack the system to access the files found in the ship's protected database. It required some overclocking to achieve this. Something else popped in the process, making one of his eyes blink repeatedly.

Eventually, he broke through the system defences and started to search the files. He inspected the prisoner data, finding details of many different captives. It seemed that the Raetuumaka didn't just scavenge technology. They took the crew as well. Groups of prisoners were assigned different symbols, many of which Ontri was able to decipher. The one with a man of Skip's description, the only human prisoner they had, was in the Dozen Deaths category. Ontri mused on that for a moment. His rather limited understanding was that one death was usually enough.

"Block 187-G," Ontri said aloud, reading the location of Skip's cell. He didn't need to read aloud, but he'd seen many humans do it, and presumed it was a good thing.

He removed the port connecting him to the console and smiled at a passing Raetuumak engineer. He wasn't aware that he was still constantly winking.

"Just charging up," he said in Raetuum.

"You should report to maintenance."

"Why, thank you. I shall."

Ontri had seen humans telling their children it never hurt to have manners, to always use their "p's and t's," as they put it. He found it all rather enthralling, and found that on most occasions it worked. On others, violence worked wonders.

His vision went suddenly, then came back. He felt a little different. His damaged fault detection couldn't tell what the problem was, but his "gut," as humans called it, told him a chip had shut down. He wasn't sure what that chip was, but made a mental note to attend maintenance and request an assessment. If they wouldn't help, he could always kill them.

Ontri finished processing that task, then turned his attention to the next one: finding the cell and freeing Skip. He used the computer's system to calculate the fastest route, making note of checkpoints along the way.

Throughout his wandering, which still took longer than predicted, he thought he heard a lot of shouting and gunfire. He presumed it was just another fault in his hardware, and wondered if this was what humans meant by "getting old," or "dying." He wondered if he should start processing regrets.

He arrived on the floor where Skip's cell was located. According to the computer, there should have been a patrol here, but it seemed the guards were sleeping. One of them appeared to be smoking while he slept. Ontri made a tiny note of the potential fire risk.

He skipped down towards the cell. "Good sir!" he cried. "I've come to rescue you!"

He reached the bars and saw the gate ajar. He tapped it with one finger, and it swung open. There was not a soul in sight.

"Oh," he said.

40
Rendezvous

It took some time for the Bridge to travel back to where the rest of the starship Gemini was parked, still skirting the rim of the galaxy. Skip was hesitant to cross the barrier of the warning signs—not because they were warnings (there were many others he never heeded), but because of the dark feeling in his gut that he had already been out here, that the gap in his memory was matched by the void of the Unknown.

He docked the ship, and both he and Maggie returned to their respective crews, who seemed as divided as ever. Both crews had come up with a variety of wildly-conflicting plans, and the absence of their leaders meant there was no one there to temper them. It seemed that there had been many arguments while they were gone.

"Good to see you back," Larsman said to Skip. They placed a hand on each other's shoulder, bowing their heads together. They hadn't known each other that long, but what they had been through was tough, and their mutual admiration was clear. A lot went unsaid, because speaking it was more painful than any hurt of battle.

"Fill me in," Skip said. "And ... where's Ontri?"

"I was actually going to ask you that. We thought he was captured with you."

"I went aboard the Ark alone."

"Well … when we got the Offspring back, he wasn't on board."

"Damn it," Skip said. "He's probably still on the Ark then."

"We might have to assume the worst."

"We won't assume anything. Tell me what you've come up with. We need to take out that vessel."

"We've looked at the options," Larsman said, "and the best we've come up with is firing every missile we've got from afar, then warping out of here to avoid the blast."

Skip shook his head. His distinctive solitary curl quivered. "But that won't just blow up the ship. It'll take the entire system, and probably the neighbouring ones too."

"That's the price that'll have to be paid."

"No."

"It's either that or let them go where they please."

"We can't ignore them. They're heading to the Alpha system."

"Stars. All the more reason to take them out now."

"Oh, we'll take them out, but we have to do it in a way that doesn't annihilate everyone and everything out here."

Larsman scrunched up his mouth. "Wouldn't be such a bad thing, I think. Maybe there's no room for rats in space. You saw how bad they are."

"And I saw what's driving the leash. They're not all bad, Larsman. What's ruling them is."

"What's that?"

"The Umbra, Larsman. The Umbra are back. Maybe when our parents told us those horrible bedtime stories, we didn't just shiver because they were scary, but because deep down in our heart of hearts, we knew they were real."

41
choices

Maggie didn't return to the control room of her ship. She went straight to her quarters, taking off her power armour to start repairs. There was something comforting in getting out the engineering equipment, in focusing all her energy—and all her mind—on something practical. It was something she could change. Something she could fix.

Lieutenant Toz, unable to leave anything alone, knocked on her door. She knew it was him by his knock. He liked to make a little song out of the raps. He had a tendency to tap out a beat on his rifle too. Said it helped him concentrate. She guessed it was his equivalent of fixing things.

"Come in," she said, though really she meant "Go away." She couldn't say how she felt, because she was still trying to keep up appearances, still trying to be the ship's commander. For so long, she looked down on Skip, even mocked him for all the cracks she saw in him. Now, after everything she knew he'd been through—and some she only guessed about—she wondered how he hadn't broken apart entirely. For the first time since boarding the Gemini, she started to realise this really was a punishment, and that some people, maybe not her, didn't deserve it. She started to realise that by the end of her galaxy service, she might have cracked as well.

Toz came in, but not fully. He stood by the door awkwardly, resting against the frame. He scratched his greasy hair for a moment, saying nothing.

"Well?" Maggie asked.

"Eh, uh, I just … I'm glad you're safe, Maggie."

Maggie couldn't bring herself to thank him. Not everyone was safe. Not everyone came back. There might have been celebrations on both rockets—on Gemini Left more than anything—but she didn't consider this a victory at all. To her, the mission was a failure.

"And I, uh," Toz continued, "just wanted to say sorry."

"For what?"

"How I acted before."

"Forget about it."

"It's just … this place. This prison. I've never been cooped up for so long. It just … it just got to me."

"I get it," Maggie said, still working away on her power armour. "And I'm sorry too."

"Why are you sorry? You got him back. You were right."

"I'm sorry I got you landed with this. The galaxy service was the best I could get, or so I thought. I thought maybe it was a way out … but really it's just a prison without bars."

"We'll get out in time," Toz said. "Only a few more big discoveries."

She suspected he didn't really believe it, that he

was just putting on a brave face for her benefit.

"I'm not so sure about that," Maggie replied. "We lost Alex."

"Alex? The Primus boy?"

"Yeah."

"What do you mean we lost him?"

"He snuck aboard the Bridge. He's dead, Toz. The kid is dead."

She looked back at her equipment. She didn't want to see Toz's reaction. He knew well what Alex's death meant. They couldn't go back to Empire territory without having to pay a price for that. Skip's crew sure wouldn't pay it, even though the teen was under their watch. It'd be the ragtag band of outlaws on Gemini Right. No matter how much they pretended to be scientists, they'd still be seen as criminals. Whenever anything went wrong, they'd be blamed for it too.

"Let's not go back then," Toz suggested.

"What?"

"We're out here beyond the Edge. Maybe we can live out here."

"But I have a life back home."

"You *had* a life, Maggie. It won't be waiting for you when this all ends."

Maggie sunk her head. It was getting harder to focus on her repairs. She was starting to make mistakes. She supposed she'd started making them a long time ago. The biggest one was getting caught. Right now, there was no real reason to go home. There was no reason to save an Empire she didn't believe in, and one that certainly didn't believe in her. She could bow out now, go on the run, like so many other enemies of the Empire did, and maybe carve out some kind of living along the Edge. She sighed, knowing that she couldn't live that life.

"That space barge is heading for the Alpha system," she said. "That's where it'll blow."

"Then let it. Let them have it. We don't owe them anything, Maggie. And stars, maybe it's better if the Empire falls. What good has it done us? We know there's corruption there. We know they've been hiding devastating weapons. Maybe this is ... I don't know, cosmic justice."

"We can't just let them die," Maggie said.

"We were supposed to make discoveries, Maggie, not fight a war."

"Well, this is one discovery."

"They won't thank us for it, you know."

"I know."

"Then why bother saving them?"

"Because some things are worth doing even if there's no reward."

42
good advice

Skip retired to his quarters, feeling he was due a much-deserved rest, but knowing quite well that he'd have a hard time sleeping. More than anything, he needed advice. He needed guidance. If there was anyone who could give that to him, it was his long-serving companion, Lieutenant Fellow.

"Boy am I glad to see you," Skip said, as soon as he entered his quarters. Just as much as he could count on Ontri's support, he could count on finding Lieutenant Fellow to be found in their shared quarters, working tirelessly on his war strategies.

Lieutenant Fellow said nothing. He was the quiet type, reserved, only leaving his quarters at night when most of the other crew were sleeping. You might have said he essentially lived in that room, and no one bothered him about it all, least of all Skip.

"I see you've been working away," the Captain said, looking around the room. There were papers strewn about the place, some on the tables, many on the floor. Lieutenant Fellow was messy, to say the least, but that didn't matter when he was such good counsel.

"I'm torn, Lieutenant," Skip said, sitting down

across from him. He let out a terrible sigh. "I really don't know what to do. I feel like I've stumbled into something that we weren't supposed to. We've got no backup out here. It's just us. We're out of communications range with the Empire."

The two exchanged glances.

"Yeah, I know," Skip said. "I guess the path is clearer than I think it is. It just isn't an easy path. But then … I guess they're never easy, huh? Everyone's gotta make a sacrifice some time. Maybe this is ours."

Lieutenant Fellow continued to give the Captain his full attention. He mightn't have been much of a talker, but he was a damn good listener. Sometimes that was all Skip needed.

"I need to know though," Skip continued. "Do we blow it all up, or do we try to take over this thing and disarm it from the inside? That kind of sounds like suicide, but maybe that's better than all the killing the first option involves."

He stood up and headed over to Lieutenant Fellow, who sat on his chair, staring at him. Skip patted the Lieutenant's head. He always liked that. It made him more amenable to giving advice.

Skip took a little ship down from a display shelf and plopped it in the centre of the table. Lieutenant Fellow stared at it intently, but didn't budge while Skip kept his hand around the ship's base.

"Let's say this is the space barge," Skip said. "And the table is the galaxy."

Lieutenant Fellow purred in agreement.

"So, do we knock it off the table, or do we take it for our own?"

Skip moved his hand away, and Lieutenant Fellow hopped from his seat and landed on the table. He grabbed the ship in his mouth, then brought it back to his chair, where he tapped it with his paws.

"I knew I could count on you," Skip said, petting the cat. "You've guided me through many wars. Let's hope your advice holds up, Lieutenant. Maybe then you'll be up for promotion."

43
a plan of action

Skip and Maggie arranged a meeting with the highest ranking members of both crews. They met in the Bridge. That was their default space for arranging compromises. It wasn't any surprise that they didn't meet there often.

"We have a plan," Skip said.

"Finally," Admiral Mendan croaked. He sat in the pilot seat, gripping the control panel, seeming as ready to get in on the action as anyone else. He strained his eyes at the viewscreen. "Just don't get in the way of my guns," he warned.

"You're not fighting," Maggie said.

"You think I'm too old, huh?" He struggled up and started pointing to each of them in turn. "You all thought I was mad, you did. Well, I was right! They came back. I kept tellin' ya. No one'd listen. And will that starspanker Nebula write about this, huh?"

"Right, calm down," Skip said. "We need your strategic mind more than ever, Admiral."

"Damn right ya do!" Mendan hammered his index finger at his temple. "Never lost a single marble! Not so sure about the rest o' you."

"The plan," Maggie said, nudging Skip.

"Yeah," Ken Danris, Skip's Marine trainer, barked. He was a Bulker, with more muscle than the rest of the people there combined. Him in power armour was a sight to behold. He was pretty eager to get into some now. "I want me some fightin'." He was never a man of many words, but what few he used worked wonders on rallying the soldiers. He'd make you believe you could shoot down anything. All you needed was the right gun.

"We can't shoot down the Ark," Skip said. "We need to take it over."

"Won't it be just as dangerous in Empire hands?" Toz asked. Those were treasonous words, and some of Skip's crew grumbled at them. Toz was lucky he was out of earshot of the Emperor.

"The chance of that barge being captured by someone else out here is high," Skip said. "It flies too slow. We'd have to accompany it for years to get it back to Empire territory. We can't risk someone else getting their hands on it."

"So, what do you propose?"

Maggie stepped up. "We're going to scuttle it."

"What a waste," Larsman said.

"In any other circumstance," Mendan said, "I'd agree. But the Umbra are out here. They'll be bending the ears of every species across the rim, until they all call them Masters. We can't let a weapon like this exist out here. It has to be dismantled."

"How do we even do that?" Larsman asked.

"We've got to board it and take it from the inside," Skip said.

"That's suicide!"

"We've done it already."

"Yeah, by stealth."

"Well, now let's do it by storm."

"We can do this," Maggie said, "with our combined crews. We've got all the tools we need."

"We've got a lot of weaponry," Skip said.

"Oooh yeah!" Danris cheered.

"The problem," Skip continued, "is that they've got weapons we've got no defences for. They use psychic abilities. They call them Mind-killers."

"Psy-soldiers," Admiral Mendan mused, chewing his lip.

"Yeah," Skip said. "I guess you could call them that."

"I've fought them before. Hmph! Was told I was mad for that too."

"No one thinks you're mad now," Maggie said.

"*Now*, yes. Well, I wouldn't worry about those Mind-killers. I've got just the weapon to fight them."

44
a one-man army

Admiral Mendan led the team to his quarters, to the glass container that so many had dismissed as one of the admiral's odd-ball trophies. He had a lot of other strange artefacts from bygone wars, and it was all taken to be largely a show of past glories, likely for the benefit of the Galaxy Express journalist, and, through him, the galaxy as a whole.

They were wrong.

After some time pressing his face close to the controls on the cylinder, grumbling to himself as he tried to make out which button was which, the admiral drained the liquid out. They all stared in silence for a moment, waiting for something to happen. They thought maybe Mendan had developed an anti-psy-soldier toxin from the female body inside, that the liquid would be poured into needles and weapons.

Then the woman moved.

They gasped, and some flinched.

She opened her eyes, and they seemed to be blue, and then with a blink, green, and then with another, brown. So it seemed that they kept changing, including colours no human had ever seen before. And there was something about her stare, something hypnotic. Her hair was ghostly white, and her skin ghostly pale, which made the ever-shifting colours of her eyes stand out even more.

Mendan opened the glass door, letting the woman step out. She was almost entirely naked, but seemed to have no concern about it. Some of those attending weren't sure whether to stare or look away.

"Admiral," she said. Her voice was haunting. It seemed to come from far off and very close at the same time, like she was speaking from across the galaxy and yet whispering to their very ears. There was also the hint of many voices, and her accent was difficult to pin down.

"This is the body of Glacia Andros, one of my finest soldiers," the admiral explained.

"The body?" Skip asked.

"Inside," Mendan said, "are the rest of her division. Or their minds, at least."

Many there were dumbfounded. They had so many questions, they weren't sure what to ask.

"We are a hundred minds," the woman said. "Once divided, like you. Now united."

Everyone there, bar perhaps Mendan, felt a little woozy. The way she talked and stared at them seemed to be having an effect like a trance. It was difficult to concentrate, and it seemed whenever they did have the mental power to do so, it was largely through her allowing it to happen.

"So, you're our weapon," Skip said, wondering if that was offensive.

"All minds are weapons," she replied. "Ours are a weapon one hundred times the power."

"You can fight the Mind-killers though, right?"

"We can already feel their minds from across the expanse. Yes, we can fight them."

"Good," Skip said, feeling more confident about this mission.

Larsman cleared his throat. "Are you, eh, gonna fight in *that*?" He pointed to the thin piece of fabric around her waist, barely hiding anything at all.

"For your comfort, we will attire this shell of flesh with a shell of fabric."

"Good. It's just ... eh ... might be a distraction is all."

She smiled. "Some minds are easily distracted."

"So, what do we call you?" Skip asked.

"There are no names entirely appropriate, but for your convenience, you may call us by the name formerly associated with this body, our host: Glacia."

"And, uh, what about ... you know?"

"My sex?"

Skip blushed. "Yeah."

"I have a female body, though it is changing, so for your comfort and convenience, you may call us 'she', though 'they' is much more accurate. We are female and male, and everything between, and in that union we may perhaps have discovered a third, more androgynous form. We are all, and beyond all." She looked at Skip intensely. "We are the future, though it scares you."

45
bedtime stories

There was no delay. Once everyone was assigned their duty—and given instructions for what to do if it all went wrong—they set out to find and disarm the Ark. Some of them weren't the fighting type, but they had no choice. The crew of starship Gemini, so often divided, would go into this together. It was just a pity they wouldn't all come out of it together too.

Maggie helped Skip load up the fighters. That included new missiles. She didn't pretend she was happy about it, but she was beginning to think there might not be a way of doing this without a lot of weapons fired—and at least some people killed.

"Why didn't you tell them about that thing on board?" Maggie asked. It was just the two of them, so she could speak freely. The rest of the crew were busy with their own preparations.

Skip hesitated. "I didn't want to scare 'em."

"But they need to know."

"No," Skip said. "They need to take over the ship. *We* need to kill the Umbra."

"Do we even know how?"

"I consulted with Lieutenant Fellow about it."

"And?" She was going to ask why she'd never met

the Lieutenant that Skip so often talked about, and why he wasn't on the crew register, but she decided against it. She had a feeling the illusive strategist might have been a government spy. The less she got on his radar, the better.

"We went over the old bedtime stories for clues."

"You might not want to tell the crew that."

"Why not?"

Maggie raised her eyebrows. "Well, we're going to war, and here you are reading children's stories with your chief strategist. Doesn't look right."

"It doesn't have to look right. It just has to *be* right."

"But … can we rely on those?"

"It's the only information we have," Skip said. "I'm starting to think the Empire destroyed any true records, that the only way for our ancestors to ensure the information would be passed on was through stories."

"So, what did you find?"

"There's a recurring trend in many of the tales."

"Yes?"

"The only way to destroy shadow is with light."

46
warp drop

There was one way to really take an enemy by surprise, and that was by dropping from warp speed right on top of them. The Gemini appeared in the blink of an eye, cruising over the space barge. By the time the Raetuumaka picked it up on their radar, it split apart.

The rockets, controlled by the ever-ambidextrous Larsman, took position parallel to the Ark, ready to fire or draw fire, and ready to use new enhancements Cada had come up with to link the boosters to the Infinite engines, letting them turn quicker than before.

The Offspring, flown by Skip, and carrying Glacia, Danris, and an assortment of armoured Marines, flew along overhead, making for the front of the vessel. Skip was getting more and more into "the red zone," as the Marines called it, thanks to Danris leading a battle verse with a call and response. "We are going to the war!" the Bulker sang, answered by the others with: "So count your kills, and kill some more!"

The Bridge, flown by Maggie, and carrying Toz, Cada, and another Marine battalion, flew under the Ark, coasting along the hull, close to the shields. Toz had his favourite sniper rifle ready. Cada had her toolboxes—one on her back, three small ones attached to her belt, and one more in each hand. The Marines did their own chant, but it wasn't quite as boisterous as on the other ship.

The gunfire came in flurries, back and forth between all the vessels. Gunners aboard Gemini Left took pocket shots at the shields, enough to draw the ire of the enemy. The hangars of the Ark opened, and their fighters came out by the dozen. Right on cue, just as Skip predicted. It meant less Raetuumaka inside the space barge to deal with.

Gemini Right drew the gunfire of the Ark's starboard side, unable to shoot back, but able to take a beating. When the enemy stopped wasting ammunition against those reinforced shields, Larsman tried a new tactic: diving nose first into the enemy, making their own shields quiver, and turning their gunners' attention back to the defence-heavy rocket. To some, it seemed like a waste to draw fire from both sides of the barge, but that was all part of the plan. It kept the enemy busy, kept them distracted from the real threat posed by the two boarding parties.

When fighting a wild animal, many warriors would say to strike the underbelly, where it's weakest. That was exactly where Maggie went, skirting the underside of the barge, using her array of scanners (some moved from Gemini Right to the Bridge) to identify the weakest part of the shields and hull. Then she pounced, firing the Shield Buster that she had saved from previous battles. It punched a hole in the shields. She followed it with a volley of missiles, which rent a hole in the hull. Then all she had to do was push hard on the accelerator. The fighter-bomber cruised through the two openings, crashed through a corridor, and skidded to a halt in one of the Raetuumaka crew quarters. Debris crumbled, dust scattered and exposed wires sparked.

"Well," Toz said, cranking his rifle. "I guess we make our own landing bay."

47
mind games

Skip wished he had a Shield Buster, but when one big punch wouldn't do the job, a lot of little punches might. He kept a steady rattle of laser fire at the shields, interspersed with torpedoes, until he saw it start to flicker out. It took almost everything the fighter had, leaving no missiles to breach the hull. He'd just have to cut through that manually.

He clamped the fighter to the top of the barge, far away from the stacks of crates magnetically bound to the surface. He didn't want a stray laser to hit one of those and start a chain explosion. That chain wouldn't end until several planets went up too.

They suited up, all except Glacia, who insisted that she did not need armour or machinery to survive in the vacuum of space, or in any other environment. All she needed was her mind. Indeed, she didn't feel she even needed clothes, but she wore a leather suit for their sake. For the rest of them, Platinum Grade power suits were the uniform of choice. Danris unsealed the outer hatch, then trudged up to the space barge's hull. He activated the power saw on his left arm, cutting through the metal. He had to cut a very big hole for him to fit through.

The group, dubbed Team Mindrock, stepped aboard the Ark.

The Raetuumaka were waiting.

The initial blasts came fast and heavy. Unlike the surprise appearance of Maggie on a lower level below, the enemy detected Skip's barrage of missiles against their shields, knowing exactly where he would enter. A large contingent of Raetuumaka soldiers were perched behind makeshift barriers, guns at the ready.

The bulk of Danris drew much of their fire. Then the other Marines stepped forward, hauling out their two-handed flak guns. They sprayed the room with gunfire, forcing many of the Raetuumaka to duck for cover. That was when Skip leapt into the fray, getting up close and personal, taking some of them out with a gun to the head—others with a gauntleted fist.

Yet there were so many Raetuumaka that even Skip couldn't fight or see them all. One of them pointed a blaster at his helmet at point blank range. Then Glacia stepped forward, placing her hand on the Raetuumak's shoulder.

"You will fight for us now," she said.

And, much to the surprise of the others, the Raetuumak turned around and started firing on his kin.

"Wow," Skip said. "I'm sure glad they don't have you."

"They are weak-minded."

"Yeah."

"But then so are most humans."

She walked ahead. Skip wasn't sure if she meant him.

Team Mindrock pressed on, clearing out the next hall, and then the next, pushing back the enemy. More reinforcements came, and Skip was glad. The more of them there were up here, the less of them were downstairs with Maggie. He only hoped the Umbra wasn't down there instead.

They encountered another set of guards ahead. The Marines ploughed through many of them, while Glacia casually strolled towards them, seemingly averting their gunfire. She placed her hand on the shoulder of that group's commander, repeating her enchanting words. While the Raetuumak seemed in shock, he didn't turn his weapon on his comrades.

"This one has a stronger mind," she told Skip when he approached. He was about to respond when she added, "No matter." Blood leaked from the Raetuumak's eyes, ears, nose, and mouth. Then he toppled over, dead.

"Stars!" Skip cried. "I'm *really* glad they don't have you."

"Maybe save some of that juju for the psy-soldiers," Danris said.

She continued on, unfazed. For the Marines, it really did seem like some kind of paranormal power, but Skip had a feeling that Glacia didn't see it that way. It was simply the power of the mind, the most potent weapon available to them all.

48
back on board

The hatch doors of the Bridge opened. A group of Raetuumaka guards approached hesitantly. They were right to be hesitant. Before they could hit their triggers, Toz took each of them out with a volley of sniper fire. The bodies slumped on top of one another.

The Marines trotted out, guns at the ready. Then Maggie came next, back in her defence-heavy power suit, this time with a hand-held energy shield for added measure. Behind her was Cada, the engineer who Maggie knew would be pivotal in taking control of this ship.

They advanced, slow and careful. Unlike Skip's role, this group, dubbed Team Hushwire, wasn't meant to bulldoze through soldiers. It was meant to break into the ship's systems.

Cada set up her gear at the nearest port, loading up a ton of cables. Maggie knew what some of them were, but not all of them. It seemed like some Cada had designed herself, to get faster bandwidths than conventionally possible. The Marines looked at each other dumbly, and back to their weapons. At least they knew those really well.

"This is going to take some time," Cada said.

"Take as long as you need," Maggie replied.

"Not too long," Sergeant Kast, leader of their Marine force, said. To say that he was on edge was an understatement. There was something about these kind of missions, the silent and sneaky ones, that rattled the nerves. Every stray sound or darting shadow seemed like something more.

Maggie used the time to recharge her shields, and to power up some battery packs she made the Marines carry on their backs. If she had to, she'd turn her mission into a ten-hour siege defence. She just hoped she wouldn't need more than ten.

She also started a search for Ontri. She picked up what she thought was his signal a few times, but then it dropped again. She wasn't sure if that was a fault of her scanners, the barge's systems, or Ontri himself. It made her worry. A big part of the plan rested on getting Ontri back—and getting him in working order.

All these accesses of the space barge's systems would have been flagged in the control room, but Maggie used node redirection to cloak her tracks. Whenever the intrusions came up, they seemed like they were coming from different parts of the ship. Often, it seemed like they were coming from the top levels, where Team Mindrock were rampaging. She knew Skip had no issue with her sending more foes his way.

"Got it," Cada said. "We should have transmission coming in now."

The comms system throughout the vessel kicked in. A signal transmitted from the antennae and broadcasting dishes that lined the hull of Gemini Right. It was in the Raetuum tongue, or as best an approximation the Gemini Right linguists could achieve. It told the Raetuumaka that they were being controlled by a hostile power, that they should lay down their arms and surrender, or rise up against their oppressors. It told them that it wasn't worth dying in a futile fight against those with superior firepower, and that the cargo of their vessel was meant to destroy worlds, just like theirs.

Skip would fight the war of bodies, but Maggie's team would fight the war of minds. She hoped that they would listen to reason. Even Skip, with enough pressure, listened to reason now. She hoped that the Raetuumaka would see her message as the truth, and that less of them would die.

She also hoped the message wouldn't draw out that oppressor the broadcast spoke of, the Umbra. She didn't put too much faith in that hope, because reason told her that it would.

49
conventional
weapons

The Raetuumaka might have swarmed like rats, but they fell like flies. Against the armour, weaponry, and training of the Pan-Galactic Marines, they were destined to take a beating. With Skip Sutridge, General Extraordinaire, leading that force, they didn't stand a chance.

The Raetuumaka's best defence wasn't their under-trained warriors, but rather the ship itself. When they started to flee on a massive scale, they sealed behind every room and corridor they could. Skip couldn't pick up Ontri from his location—and he hoped it wasn't because of something worse. He also didn't have the mathematical mind of Maggie, or the engineering skill of Cada, so hacking through the control pads wasn't going to work.

It was lucky, then, that Danris was a Bulker, because he was able to carry one of the biggest hand-held guns they had: the Shatterer. This colossal weapon, which required several of the other Marines to prop themselves up against Danris to stop him from toppling over, was a sonic boomer, capable of sending ultra-sonic waves that could rip through metal. He loaded it up, letting it charge. It might have been powerful, but it was damn slow. Skip kept a lookout while it was loading.

Then Danris fired. It was like an earthquake. You could feel it through your armour, and hear it through the protective ear muffs the accompanying Marines were issued with. Some were known to have gone deaf from a sonic blast. Others suffered brain damage. Skip had an ounce of pity for any Raetuumaka holed up behind the next wall.

The blast left a hole in the next room, and the next, and several more down the corridor. One of them was where many Raetuumaka prisoners were being kept. Some of them fled, while others cowered in the ruins. It seemed that some were too far gone to flee. Yet one of those who hopped through the hole and started to scurry away looked very familiar.

"El-erae!" Skip cried.

The Raetuumak halted and glanced around.

"Human," she replied. "I … I forgot your name."

She scampered over, placing her hand on Skip's arm. "You survived the Dozen Deaths," she said. "Or … I didn't."

Glacia stepped forward, placing her hand on El-erae's shoulder.

"Stars, no!" Skip yelled, pulling Glacia's hand away. "She's an ally."

"Ally might be stretching it," El-erae said. "Fellow sufferer, more like."

"She has a very strong mind," Glacia observed.

"You need one if you are to face the Dozen

Deaths."

Glacia smiled. "How about a hundred?"

"El-erae," Skip said. "How does taking over this vessel sound?"

"It sounds delicious."

"Oh, it is. But first, you wouldn't happen to know where they keep the weapons they take from prisoners? My tags are with my armour. Let's just say they're more than a little … sentimental."

"Come then," El-erae said. "I know where they store scavenged weapons. My own will be there too."

El-erae led them through a maze of corridors, hacking through some of the controls. Danris grumbled as she did. He rather liked using the Shatterer. In time, they found themselves in the vessel's main weapons storeroom, filled high with all sorts of equipment. Skip found his old power suit there, recovering his dog tags. One of them had been given to him by General Felvin Oxlis, a hero of his as a child. Another was given by the Emperor. He didn't care so much about that.

El-erae gave out an excited squeal as she plucked her old weapon from the stack. From a first glance, and then a second, it looked like a wooden staff.

"A stick," Skip said, blinking. "This is your weapon. A stick."

"You do know people use blasters now?" Danris told her. "Or sonic boomers."

"In the hands of the untrained, it is just a stick. To the Olruuana, it is the finger of the Blinking Gods." She lashed it at one of the blasters in the pile, cracking the gun in half. "Pray it doesn't touch you!"

50
mind-killer

Team Mindrock continued pushing back the enemy on the top level, but this time El-erae joined the fight. She was a bit like Maggie in that she had no desire to kill—least of all her kin—but she had no qualms with causing severe injury. A swipe of her staff was enough to break bones. Even with the muted sounds Skip heard inside his power suit, the cracks made him cringe.

They were about to descend to the next level when they were faced with As-hamaz and two other Mind-killers. Skip could feel them before they even appeared, and it seemed like they appeared from nowhere, as if they had previously cast a cloak into his mind, which they only now removed.

There was a feeling of a great weight upon all minds, but it seemed that the strain was noticed most by Glacia. She clenched her fists and gritted her teeth, keeping her eyes on the trio of Mind-killers before her. Up to now, it had been easy. Admiral Mendan had always warned his soldiers not to get cocky, but Glacia didn't listen before. It took everything she had to push back against the psy-soldiers, to weaken their manipulative mind rays before they hit her comrades.

"So," As-hamaz said, and the word seemed to burrow into Skip's mind. "You have come back to obey the law of the Dozen Deaths."

Skip raised his flak rifle. "Only if it's you who's dyin'."

"Put that away, child."

To Skip's great surprise, he did.

"We broke you," As-hamaz said. "Let us put you back together as we see fit."

Danris scoffed. "Want me to boom 'em?" he asked Skip, pulling the sonic boomer from his back. The accompanying Marines raced over to prop him up.

"Oh, yes," As-hamaz said. "Make the second one death by sound."

Just as Danris had almost finished powering up the Shatterer, he turned it on Skip and El-erae.

"No!" Skip cried. He dived one way, while El-erae hopped and rolled off to the other, landing on her feet with a jump.

The sonic blast tore through the wall to the next room, and tore a chunk off the side of Skip's helmet as he ducked to the ground. It was lucky it didn't tear a chunk out of his head as well. He felt the sound inside his brain, inside his chest, inside his heart. His entire body shook, and he had just gotten the edge of the blast. If he hadn't dived, he would have been torn apart.

Skip could barely move. He couldn't get up. Danris was charging up the weapon again.

Some of the Marines tried to fire on the Mind-killers, but As-hamaz got them to turn their weapons on each other. Glacia probed their minds just in time to tell them to jump out of the way of the gunfire, until the Marines lay in a pile on the ground, bewildered.

El-erae dove and span, whirling about with her staff. She struck the ankle of one of the Mind-killers with a crack. The Raetuumak screamed out and fell to the floor, but before El-erae could move in for a second strike, the force of the Mind-killer's scream was amplified by a psychic wave, knocking her back to the ground.

El-erae's attack gave an opening for Glacia. She pushed hard, though they pushed back. The force of the psychic blows was physically evident. They literally moved across the floor, digging their feet in as they tried to hold their ground. Gusts of what seemed like wind threw back their hair or fur, and pulled the skin back on their faces. One moment it blew one way, and the next the other. This mental tug of war played out with Danris also. Glacia turned him towards the Mind-killers, and they turned him back towards Skip, who still struggled to get up from the ground. The supporting Marines shimmied along with the Bulker, their minds equally caught in the net.

The next sonic wave passed as Danris switched targets, missing both. As-hamaz's mental prowess was like nothing Glacia had experienced before. In it, she sensed a link to a darker, more powerful force: the Umbra.

Skip watched as Glacia was brought to her knees, as she was weakened, just like him. She struggled to push back, to fight off the attacks on all of their minds, but even with a hundred of her own, it was not enough.

Skip had fallen, and was of no use on the ground.

Don't you damn fall, the admiral had told him. Well, he'd fallen before. When he was crossing those bars as a child, and all those taunts and jeers came at him like missiles, he fell. He'd been through life, and he'd stumbled along the way. But he always got back up. He always tried again.

So now, he searched for that unrelenting part of him, and when he found it, he told himself to get up. Sometimes someone else would pull you to your feet, but he'd learned well that more often than not you had to push yourself up.

He struggled up and turned to As-hamaz. If there was one thing he could count on, it was the hatred that had festered inside him any time he saw that furry face. As-hamaz wanted to break him, wanted him not just to fall, but never get back up. He wanted him to kneel, but he was the Man Who Didn't Kneel. He wanted him to cry, but he was the Man of No Tears.

He hobbled forward, grabbing his gun. One step, then two.

Then the wave of mental pain came upon him like a pouncing predator. He was momentarily paralysed. His body still shook from the vibrations of the sonic blast. His breath was fleeting. His sight was strained. Everything was a struggle. But then, that was life.

He pushed on, through the barrier. Another step, another fall. He got back up, but was brought down again. Yet even his attempts, feeble though they might have seemed, gave strength to those around him. El-erae took out the second of the Mind-killers with her flips and swipes. Glacia renewed her pushback against As-hamaz's never-ending siege.

"Stay down!" As-hamaz shouted at him.

Skip fell to one knee, and felt the other buckling. The pain was excruciating, as much in his body as his mind. Unlike El-erae or Glacia, he couldn't separate the two.

"No!" he yelled back, like he yelled to those Alphan children. His hair was affray, pushed back by the force of the mental assault, all but that little golden curl of defiance.

He got back up, pushing on, taking the pain and using it to drive his feet forward like a whip. He could feel the veins bulge in his neck. He could feel his eyes bulge in his head. He clenched his teeth so hard that his jaw ached.

"Down!" As-hamaz bellowed. The strain was now evident on his face too. Glacia was gaining mental vigour from Skip's assault, from his undaunted willpower.

"Never!" Skip cried out, taking another painful step forward. He gave it his all, forcing his blaster rifle to aim at As-hamaz. He fired.

As-hamaz gasped and stumbled back. The wave of mental aggression continued, but it was suddenly halved in power.

"One death," Skip said, breathing heavily. He fired again.

As-hamaz fell to his knees, wheezing.

"Two!" Skip blurted, spitting out the word, letting his anger guide him. He fired again. "Three!"

As-hamaz fell over, but struggled back up just as quick, leaning on one arm. Skip fired at it.

"Four!" he yelled. "How many more deaths?"

As-hamaz cried out, clutching his blasted arm as he collapsed to the floor. Skip blasted the other one.

"Five!" he shouted. "How many do you *deserve*?"

He fired another six blasts in quick succession, until his gun was out of charge.

"Six! Seven! Eight! Nine! Ten! Eleven!" he cried. He was overcome by emotion. He realised this wasn't just about As-hamaz. It was about everything. There were buried memories from his "missing year," when he disappeared from Empire territory. He didn't know what they were. Just like the Umbra, they were shrouded in shadow.

As-hamaz writhed about on the floor, moaning and shaking. He should have been dead. Eleven blasts at this range would have killed most species, but it seemed this Raetuumak had a strength of body as well as mind. Skip didn't care. It meant he could kill him again.

"Well," Skip said, standing over him. "One left, huh?" He stared at the pitiful creature, feeling some compassion, but knowing that As-hamaz had none for anyone else. "How do you want to die?"

As-hamaz snarled at him. "It doesn't matter! It won't be as bad as yours!"

Skip limped over to where Danris was standing, wide-eyed. He helped turn him towards the Raetuumak, then flicked on the charger.

As-hamaz struggled to his knees, spitting blood. "They'll be … back for you … Captain!"

Before Skip could ask him what he meant, the gun fired. The blast tore through As-hamaz and the surrounding rooms, leaving just a pile of blood and metal.

El-erae offered Skip her staff to lean upon. He needed it. Glacia seemed to recover quickly now that the Mind-killers had been neutralised. The rest of them were exhausted, though it was a fight worth being exhausted after. They had won.

As-hamaz was dead.

Yet, like a ghost, Skip couldn't shake the thought of those who As-hamaz said would be back for him.

51
Inside the
Swarm

Outside the Ark, the battle raged in space. Larsman cruised past the sides of the space barge, giving a volley, before continuing on, out of the way of its answering blasts. Other times, when the flak cannons aboard Gemini Left were destroyed, he rotated the rocket, revealing another set of cannons, and then another, until it seemed that the Gemini didn't just have endless ammunition—it had endless guns to fire them.

Inside the rocket, the gunners toiled, rotating their gun positions to take out many of the approaching fighters. Admiral Mendan took up a gunner post, and he made the journalist Ted Nebula take up the one beside him.

"If you want to live, boy, you'll fight like the rest of us!"

Ted cringed as he fired. His flak cannon shook violently, shaking him with it. Tapping letters on a datapad hadn't given him the muscles he needed for such a powerful weapon, so he struggled to move it, and had to largely rely on the automated settings.

Raetuumaka fighters struggled against the superior firepower of the Gemini, so some of them resorted to desperate measures. They dived at the thrusters of the rockets, hoping to at least destroy the Infinite engines, and cripple the Gemini's means of escape. The crew had to coordinate well to keep these suicidal fighters at bay, with all reporting to Larsman of an incoming wave. He cranked the thrusters on full then, letting the intense heat break the fighters apart before the impact. It was a delicate and dangerous thing, because just one mistimed move could let a fighter through, and the Gemini crew would be stuck out there, unable to return home.

The enemy fighters went down by the dozen, but the real struggle was finding a way to take them out without striking the cargo aboard the Ark. Stray shots had already weakened the shields surrounding the massive crates of nuclear waste. The fear was very real that another few hits might expose that explosive payload and kill them all.

52
darkness and light

Maggie led Team Hushwire into the ship sewers that Skip had told her about. They used them to traverse large sections of the vessel, bypassing many of the guard positions. So far, their codename was working out. At least, they had the "hush" part down pat.

As they travelled, Maggie checked the water levels constantly, out of an abundance of caution for the Marines in their heavy suits. Some of them were armoured with power saw attachments just in case they got trapped below.

"I hope you know where you're going," Sergeant Kast said. Maggie wondered if he might have resented being assigned to her team, sneaking through the sewers like a rat.

"We're mapping the way," Maggie replied.

Kast grumbled. "Normally you send a scout ahead."

"You can be our scout if you want," Cada said. She never had much love for Marines.

"I'm a soldier," the sergeant said, "not a scout."

"Then we do it this way," Maggie stated. "This is

the quickest and safest way to the control room."

In time, Maggie started to pick up Ontri's signal more clearly, though it still flickered out periodically. They halted when it seemed like he was directly above them, though two floors up.

"Skip," she said over the comms in her suit.

"Yeah?"

"I think I found Ontri."

"Great. Patch him through to me."

"Well, that's the thing."

"What?"

"I keep losing his signal."

"Oh. Yeah. I still have you jammed. Let me see if I can get him."

He cut off.

"Skip?"

She waited. No response.

"Typical," Toz said, rolling his eyes. "We should've let Skip one-man this whole thing."

"He tried that," Maggie replied. "It didn't work."

Then Skip's voice came through, but it was broken up. She couldn't make out what he was saying.

"Skip? Skip, I can't hear you."

Then it dropped again, but this time it was different. This time, something interfered with the signal.

All eyes turned, sensing something emerging in the tunnel far ahead. Out of the shadows came a different kind of shadow: the Umbra. It turned into the form of a man, like a boogeyman of children's nightmares. Now it stalked the waking world of adults.

The Marines turned to it, guns at the ready.

"Wait," Maggie said.

They didn't like waiting. The apprehension was palpable.

"What the hell is that thing?" Kast asked.

Maggie didn't answer. She couldn't answer. The fear was lodged in her throat.

The shadowy figure stepped forward.

"We meet … in darkness," it said, its voice coming seemingly from everywhere, deep and resonant. Just like the shadow appeared to seep into everything around it, turning the water a darker black, removing the glimmer from the steel, its voice seemed to seep into their minds, filling them with terror.

"We don't want to fight you," Maggie said. She wasn't sure why she was trying to reason, when her heart told her to panic, to run. She didn't want to kill, but more than anything she wasn't sure how to kill this. Skip's ideas didn't come from a scientific text. They came from a children's book. They only got one shot at this. She didn't like that it was a gamble.

"Why are we stalling?" Kast whispered through his clenched teeth.

They all took a coordinated step back. The shadow advanced.

"We need time," Maggie whispered back. She glanced at Cada, trying desperately to clear the interference blocking Maggie's signal. They didn't just need time. They needed Ontri.

"Then do not fight," the shadow urged, and it sounded very convincing. "Simply bow down and call us your Masters. The shadow is all-consuming.

Your galaxy is in the path of the shadow's maw. It must be consumed."

They stepped back again, and the shadow advanced closer. Its wispy tendrils almost reached out to grab them.

"Can we shoot now?" Kast whispered.

Maggie looked at Cada, who shook her head.

Then the shadow darted forward, and no one questioned if they should shoot. Every Marine fired. The Umbra seemed to take no damage. It leapt into them, but Maggie charged forward, blocking the blow with her shields.

Then the shields flickered out, as if the shadow consumed that too.

"Run!" Maggie cried.

Toz fled before she even said the word. Cada ran, still trying to break through the interference and reconnect Maggie to Skip and Ontri. The Marines ran, trudging through the water, the pounding of their boots sending menacing echoes through the tunnel. They fired as they went, shooting madly behind them—hitting nothing but shadow. The bolts and bullets went through it, achieving nothing.

And Maggie ran. She'd made this run before, but now it was different. She felt like a lot more people were going to die.

The shadow pursued them. As it did, the water turned to ice.

"Skip!" Maggie cried into her comms. "Skip!"

His voice came back, crackled.

"Skip, it's here! Skip, we need help!"

The shadow pounced on the slowest Marine,

dragging him down, tearing through his armour as if it were cloth. His screams filled the tunnel, lapping at the heels of those yet to be consumed.

"Got it!" Cada cried. She cleared the comms.

"Skip!" Maggie shouted. "Get Ontri. We need those lights!"

"I'm tryin', Mags! I'm tryin'!"

That wasn't good. Everyone in the sewers was trying not to die.

Maggie heard Skip's voice as he tried to reach Ontri. Cada worked as she ran to clear up the signal. It worked, just in time for the second Marine to fall.

"Ontri!" Skip shouted.

"Good sir!" Ontri replied cheerfully. "I have come to rescue you."

"Yeah, do me a favour."

"Anything for you, good—"

"Hack the ship's systems. Get all the lights on. Full power. Stars, overload them! Take the energy from the shields, the engines, whatever."

"But sir—"

"Do it, Ontri! And fast!"

Another Marine tumbled.

"We need those lights!" Maggie bellowed.

"Processing," Ontri said, as he hacked into the systems.

"Process faster!" Skip ordered.

So Ontri overclocked himself yet again. Something else popped.

"Pro ... cess—" was all they heard.

They couldn't see what happened to him. His own systems shut down. His own lights turned out. Ontri stood still, his head bobbed forward, his shoulders slouched, his arms left dangling. If anyone tipped him on that occasion, he would have toppled over—and no amount of overclocking would brace his fall.

53
Flickering out

They couldn't see Ontri's lifeless form, but they knew they were in trouble. Another Marine fell, and then another. Each one that tumbled delayed the shadow just a little. It was horrible to think that those still alive felt a tiny piece of gladness when another second was added to their lives.

"I'm coming down!" Skip shouted through the comms.

"No, Skip," Maggie said. "Get to the control room. Scuttle this ship!"

They arrived at a part of the tunnel where a hatch in the ceiling was open, but they couldn't reach it. There was no ladder, nor any other means of climbing.

Kast grabbed Cada and lifted her up. "Quick!" He pushed her through the hole. Then he and two other Marines hoisted Maggie up.

"What about you?" she asked, as he pushed her through.

"What about us? Get your job done, Maggie. We've got ours."

"What about *me*?" Toz shouted from below.

"Fight like a man," Kast said, "and die like one."

"Maggie!" Toz screamed.

Maggie reached down, and Kast grabbed her hand. She pulled him up, much to the displeasure of the Marines below. Though maybe secretly, beneath that layer of disgust, some of them wished they had done the same.

"Let's kill this thing," Kast said.

He turned, and the remaining Marines turned, weapons at the ready. They shouted and fired, and then they screamed and fell.

The trio upstairs backed away from the hatch. Maggie triggered the switch to seal it up, and the doors closed slowly.

Come on, she urged. They creaked closer. *Come on!*

They shut, but they weren't the only sealed doors. The surviving members of Team Hushwire found themselves inside a small cubical room full of metal pipes. The door was firmly locked.

While Toz struggled with the handle, Cada tried to hack into the controls.

"Tell me you've got something," Maggie pleaded.

Cada shook her head. She bit her lip as she continued to bash away at the buttons.

Then the shadow bashed at the hatch doors.

"Quick, Cada!"

"I can't do anything," Cada said. "This door's manual."

Toz struggled with the door even more, wishing he was a Bulker. Maggie joined him, using the enhanced strength of her power suit. It wouldn't budge. It seemed like it was welded shut.

Then the hatch opened slowly, and up from the

sewers came the shadow. The survivors struggled with the door again. Even Cada joined them.

The shadow rose, forming again in the shape of a human. It floated across the floor towards them, slowly, reaching out, ready to consume.

Then Ontri's voice crackled on over the comms.

"I do apologise!" he said. "A momentary glitch. I have restarted my—"

"Ontri!" Maggie shouted. "The lights!"

The shadow was just inches away now. They backed away, until there was no more room to go. They closed their eyes.

Then they heard the generators kick in, and they saw a blinding light behind their eyelids. When they managed to open their eyes again, squinting, the shadow was gone. The Umbra was dead.

54
no control

To Maggie's surprise, it wasn't Skip who freed her and her companions. It was the Raetuumaka. Throughout the ship, many of them rose up against their captors, fighting with and against their kin. It was a civil war, Raetuumak against Raetuumak—not exactly what Maggie had hoped.

They led the trio through the now blinding corridors of the once dark ship, past periodic gunfire, and up to where Skip had broken into the command room with his Marines. They barricaded themselves inside as more of the opposing Raetuumaka force came their way.

No one spoke about the shadow. They were just glad that it was gone.

"You got control?" Maggie asked.

"Not exactly," Skip replied.

"Cada might be able—"

"No," Skip interjected. "We can't." He showed her the controls. It looked like they had been sabotaged. "We wanted to scuttle the ship, Mags," he added. "Well, they scuttled the controls."

"Damn," Maggie said.

Toz shrugged. "So, what, we let it float?"

"We could tow it, maybe," Cada suggested.

"What're you seeing out there, Larsman?" Skip asked.

Larsman's voice crackled on. "It's not looking good."

"Just what I thought."

"Yeah, Skip. You're on a collision course with the planet."

55
down she goes

No matter what they tried, they couldn't regain control of the ship. Even Ontri's hacking skills couldn't do it. The aut had to hole up with some rebel Raetuumaka on the other side of the ship, far from the others. He expressed no dissatisfaction about it. He was just happy to serve.

"So, we can't stop it," Skip said with a sigh.

"Not all things can be stopped," El-erae mused. "It is less painful to just accept what is."

"Yeah, unless you've got some practical wisdom, I don't wanna hear it."

"What's the best case scenario?" Cada asked.

"If we can't stop it," Maggie said, "maybe we can slow the descent."

Danris grumbled. "What good'll that do?"

"If we can land this thing without it all going off, maybe we can find a way to dismantle and bury it, somewhere no one'll find it or use it."

"There are the Endless Marshes," El-erae suggested. "Very deep. The Olruuana bring the bodies of great monks there, where the bog preserves them forever, deep and far below."

"That should stop the cargo from going off," Cada

said. "Forever, even. So long as the marshes exist, at least."

"A blink of the eye of the Blinking Gods," El-erae said.

"Will it fit the ship?" Skip asked.

"Oh, yes. And all of us."

"Yeah, I wasn't thinking about that."

"How do we guide it, though?" Toz asked. "We've got no control!"

"We've still got our ship," Maggie said. "Maybe it only needs a nudge."

"Oh, it'll need to be a careful nudge," Skip said. "This thing could still blow at any moment. And we've still got a lot of enemies on this ship."

El-erae smiled. "There is room for them in the Endless Marshes too!"

56
a gentle nudge

It didn't take long to communicate the plan to Larsman. He was up for anything, even if it did mean nudging a space barge full of nuclear cargo. If anyone had the dexterity for it, it was him.

He flew both rockets along either side of the Ark. Most of the enemy fighters were destroyed. A few were now piloted by Raetuumaka rebels, skimming the hull to take out any remaining weapons arrays.

It was a delicate job, but Larsman managed to push the rockets close enough that he essentially had the barge pinched between them. All he had to do now was go gentle with the boosters, easing a little left, then a little more. He had to pray his hand didn't twitch.

Maggie had to guide him. There were no maps of the territory, so she relied on El-erae pointing at a brownish patch of the otherwise blackened planet as an indication of just where those Endless Marshes were. Maggie passed the instructions to Larsman.

"I hope you're right," he said.

"We all hope that," Skip replied.

"I'll have to pull away before we hit the atmosphere or we might burn up the Infinite engines. We'll never get out of here then."

"Just put us on this new course," Maggie said. "We'll keep this thing from burning up."

Larsman held up his side of the bargain. With lots of careful manoeuvring, lots of tiny twists of his wrists, lots of held breaths and momentary gasps, Larsman got the Ark on a new course: heading straight into the ancient boglands that were perhaps one of the few untouched parts of the scorched planet left.

"We're closing in," he said, as they approached the atmosphere. "Time to start praying to whatever gods you believe in. I'm not sure science can help us from here."

He pulled away, letting the space barge drift down on its own, tugged now by the planet's gravity. Maggie used whatever power she could find to put up the forward shields. The space barge struck the atmosphere, cruising down.

Then the shields conked out and the ship started to crack down the middle. The crates that were magnetically stuck to the surface shuddered in place. The hull groaned. Here and there, rivets popped from their sockets and pinged across the ship. The team worked tirelessly to hold the barge together, getting the shields back on and powering up auts to fill in the widening cracks.

"That's it," Skip said. "There's nothing more we can do."

"Time to bail," Toz replied.

"I'm rooting for you guys," Larsman said. "Come back in one piece, will you?"

Then he cut out. The planet's radiation blocked the signal.

"We need to get back to the ships," Skip said.

It was a long trek to the Offspring, which still clung to the front of the vessel. They let Ontri manage the Bridge at the back, fearing they'd never make it across in time. As they clambered aboard, El-erae hesitated, looking around at the Ark that had brought her people to the stars.

"Come with us," Skip told her.

She hesitated. "But my people ..."

"We'll take as many as we can fit. We'll drop them off wherever they wanna go."

She joined them, along with two dozen more Raetuumaka rebels. On the other side of the vessel, Ontri squeezed in as many Raetuumaka into the Bridge as possible. The two fighters took off, along with many other smaller spacecraft and escape pods, leaving the Ark to its doom.

As the smaller craft passed through the atmosphere, the people on board saw the space barge descend into the Eternal Marshes, inch by inch. The swampy earth consumed it, like that all-consuming shadow of the Umbra, until there was nothing left. No one knew how deep it went, not even the Olruuana, but they hoped it was deeper than anyone could reach.

57
not so divided

The battle was won, and the exhaustion set in. They only now realised just how much their limbs ached as they stood in the decontaminators. Some had wounds that needed tending, and were sent to the medical bay on Gemini Right. Others needed a military debriefing, and were sent to Gemini Left.

El-erae stayed on the Offspring in the middle, glued to the viewscreen, watching her planet as it faded behind.

"My people," she said solemnly. "They are divided."

"Brother against brother," Toz said. "We've had that in our history too."

"And you overcame it?"

"Well, kind of. For the most part. The crew here is still pretty divided."

"At least you have shown that you can work together," El-erae said. "I take comfort in that. It gives me hope for the future of my people."

Skip was glad to be back on board the Gemini, and was glad to see that so many had survived. When he saw Ontri, he ran over to him.

"Come here, you big old tin bucket, you!"

He grabbed the aut and hugged him tightly.

"Oh," Ontri said. "Oh my. Is this … romance?"

An analysis of Ontri's systems showed up thousands of errors, many from burnt out chips. Cada was able to do some repairs, but to fix all of the problems she would have to replace Ontri's memory and personality chips. Skip wouldn't allow that.

"He's not going to be reliable," Cada warned.

Skip smiled. "He'll be more reliable than any human."

Skip found Maggie in one of her labs, cataloguing details about the Raetuumaka.

"No rest for the wicked, huh?" he asked.

She kept tapping away. "Well, you're not resting."

"I never really paid any attention to what you do down here."

"You should. It can be useful."

"I'm beginning to see that now."

"Maybe I should check out the systems on Gemini Left too," Maggie proposed.

Skip smiled. "Could be useful."

It often took a common enemy to unite two former foes. Skip and Maggie were still two very different people, sword and shield, but they had learned they worked well together. To him, her voice didn't sound quite so grating now. To her, his ego didn't seem quite so big.

The starship Gemini passed out of the Sonata system and back into the emptiness of space. The crew were confident that they would fill it with many new adventures.

THE END

ABOUT THE AUTHOR

Dean F. Wilson was born in Dublin, Ireland in 1987. He started writing at age 11, and has since become a *USA Today* and *Wall Street Journal* Bestselling Author.

He is the author of the *Children of Telm* epic fantasy trilogy, the *Great Iron War* steampunk series, the *Coilhunter Chronicles* science-fiction western series, the *Hibernian Hollows* urban fantasy series, and the *Infinite Stars* space opera series.

Dean previously worked as a journalist, primarily in the field of technology. He has written for *TechEye*, *Thinq*, *V3*, *VR-Zone*, *ITProPortal*, *TechRadar Pro*, and *The Inquirer*.

www.deanfwilson.com